The Parts I Remember

A.B. WOOD

Mentor: K. Street, KStreetauthor.com
Cover Designer: Letitia Hasser, RBA Designs
Editor: Kathleen Rothenberger
Proofreader: Judy Zweifel, Judy's Proofreading
Interior Designer: Jovana Shirley, Unforeseen Editing,
www.unforeseenediting.com

ISBN-13: 978-1718824119

To Anna and Delanie,
for holding me accountable to a word count daily.
And to my husband, for refusing to let me quit or fail.
And for always being my number one fan.

*"In vain have I struggled. It will not do.
My feelings will not be repressed.
You must allow me to tell you how ardently
I admire and love you."
~ Mr. Darcy, Pride and Prejudice*

THE CALL

H e called. It only took SIX years, THREE months, TWELVE days and some hours... BUT HE CALLED.

"How are you?"

How am I? I thought, *REALLY?? You start with THAT?? I don't even know how to answer that!* A zillion answers whirled through my mind, none of which reached my tongue. I had paused too long, and his voice came again.

"Hello?"

"I'm here."

"How are you?"

"I'm here."

Yeah, that answer was pretty accurate. I had learned to exist. To call my daily breathing "living" would be an exaggeration. I was surviving. I mean, I was okay... my world was good, I was content, but incomplete, missing a massive piece of my core, HIM.

"Can I see you?"

My heart began to race. To SEE him, to see HIM, to SEE HIM!! I had wished and prayed for this moment, every single day for years. Well... decades, actually. My heart screamed, *HELL YES*!! But I managed to gain control of my mouth, just in time to answer, coldly.

"And why would you want to do that?" *IDIOT!!* my heart screamed again, this time, scolding me.

"I'm sensing that you are upset with me." His voice trailed off...

"Don't be silly, I stopped being upset with you three years ago. These days, I simply hate you." *What the hell are you doing? Stop being hateful to him!* My heart pleading with me now.

"Oh, good," he replied as he gave a slight chuckle, "I was afraid it was gonna be bad."

*SILENCE *

"I need to see you... please? I could say it all on the phone, now, but there's so much to talk about... to explain. It would all be better relayed in person."

"Hmmmm... Why don't you give me a preview of the topic? Then I'll decide if my presence is warranted." I was still being a bitch, despite my heart's reprimands, but he had earned it after completely abandoning me all these years... and I think he knew that he deserved it. I had no doubt that he had prepared himself for it. His three-word reply, spoken in an almost desperate whisper, was the only one I would have accepted.

"I love you."

I took in a long deep breath. As I released an exhale that hinted at exasperation, I responded, while using a tone that almost implied that I was bored with the invitation.

"When and where?" But, for the first time in over six years, my heart began to fully beat again, and I felt as though I could finally breathe.

He caught me by surprise again, when he quickly responded with, "Tonight, Belle LaBlues, at eight?"

I was shocked to realize that he had flown in, or made one heck of a road trip, before making this phone call. He was HERE? Was he crazy? Traveling almost a thousand miles without a clue as to the reception he would receive? He had to be insane. What a huge gamble! What if I had said, "hell no, you jackass?" "Jackass" or "Jack" for short, had been his name for at least, the last three or four years. Even my family and friends had started using his new name whenever he would happen to come up in conversation, for whatever reason.

A smirk came to my mouth, as I considered the moment I would share that fact with him. I would not share that I had chosen to solely use his nickname, because speaking or hearing his true name... even thinking it, brought me physical pain. My inner circle thought it was just me expressing my opinion regarding him in a funny way, that also happened to agree with their view of him, after seeing the suffering he had caused me. Using it had become so natural, I would have to watch myself carefully, to keep from using it when speaking to him. This should be fun. Like a New Year's resolution to stop swearing, when it's part of your everyday vocabulary; I would be putting quarters into a "Jack" jar to break myself of the habit.

Then the realization hit me that he was here because he means business. He has no intention to be out of my life even one day longer. He was here, because he wasn't taking "no" for an answer. Or perhaps, he arrogantly thought he knew what my answer would be. He would be disappointed. I would not allow him an opportunity to hurt me ever again, regardless of how deeply I loved him. He wanted face time because he knew my soft targets, things like his deep-blue eyes and his smile. He wasn't leaving until he won. And he wanted me to have zero warning, so I would have no time to prepare a defense.

I wondered how long he had prepared to stay. What if I should choose to act stubborn? Historically, that was my style, and he had to have taken that into consideration. What about his job? What had he told his family? Not to mention, his presence here implied that he no longer had a wife... what had happened there? *It's possible that she finally saw herself in a mirror and turned into stone.* That ugly thought, pardon the pun, made me smirk. I expected answers to all my questions; detailed answers. He would be honest and hide nothing in this meeting. And he'd better bring his "A" game, because this was his only opportunity to sway me. He was "all in" at this point, and his presence here suggested that was precisely the point he wanted me to understand. I wondered if he had any idea that my trust in him was non-existent, at best. I responded again, as if I had many more things I would rather do.

"Alright, I guess. Something tells me saying no wouldn't be the end of it."

His response was smooth as silk. "That's my smart girl."

"Whatever... I'll see you at eight."

I hung up before he could say anything. I shook my head in disbelief that this moment, his return, had finally arrived, and I had really had that conversation with him. I felt like I needed to pinch myself to be sure that I was truly awake; as I had dreamed of this conversation many times.

"OUCH!"

Yep, I was awake. And in just a few short hours, I would once again lay eyes on the love of my life, the one that got away, the one I could never get over, my "Great White Buffalo." *And then I will tell him to kiss my sweet ass and to get gone*, I thought. My heart immediately responded with, *Yeah, right, ya wanna bet?*

As I stood in my closet, looking at every piece of clothing I owned, I decided to go as myself. Not done up as if to impress, just regular ol' me. My goal was to be casually dressed, but not slouchy. I chose a bright fuchsia-colored blouse because my friend Sarah had once told me that I looked beautiful in bright colors. It was cut low enough to reveal a decent rack and spark imagination, but not so low as to be considered slutty, and it had form-fitting sides, to reveal that I still had a distinct waist. I went with my favorite pair of jeans that fit just right, accentuating my curves. With me being a short girl, of only 5 feet 4 inches tall, I had an impressive collection of heels, and I chose some simple platforms that looked to be made of beige twine and cork soles. The combination worked well together, appearing casual yet classy, with just a hint of sexy. And the high heels made my butt go "POP!" *Let him get an idea of what he's missed out on, and what he can't have,* I thought.

I fixed my long, auburn hair but did not overly do it, he had not earned curls. I had never routinely colored my hair, just for fun, every so often. As the gray had begun to come in lightly and evenly distributed, from a distance you could barely notice it, at all. My hairstylist, Dusty, was sweet and always referred to them as "blonde." I went with light makeup, just a thin coat of foundation to hide some imperfections, a little eyeliner and mascara to help my green eyes stand out, and a soft hint of color on my lips, with no gloss. This made me presentable, so as not to frighten any small children, yet let my aging show... especially around my eyes. My eyes looked care-worn and tired most of the time. Still bright but missing the spark they had held before my self-professed breakdown.

All things considered, I looked pretty good, bearing in mind what I had been through mentally, in the last eight years. A recovery I would have never thought possible, in the beginning. Hours and hours, I had fought to stay mentally healthy for the greater good. I had discovered a new respect for the value of a good therapist. If only he had seen me at my worst, about six months into our most recent disconnection, I doubt he would have recognized me. I closed my eyes and shivered, as I remembered the person I had been.

Zombielike was the best description, living, but not alive. Unable to think, or feel, I had fallen into the deepest, darkest emotional hole, when Jack had abandoned me. Even though, at the time, we were nothing more than close friends, the overwhelming feeling of complete and utter despair had consumed me. I had almost taken my own life, to escape it. The darkest days had lasted for months. The shock and depression in whole, I endured for years, and still struggled with it occasionally, usually around holidays and both of our birthdays. I had lost a lot of weight, granted, that wasn't a bad thing, but it had not occurred in a healthy way. The malnutrition had caused my hair to thin and lose its shine, my skin to lose its glow and elasticity, and my muscles to become weak and even more so, from non-use. The dark circles under my eyes, from sleepless nights, had not completely faded and were a daily reminder of a time I was trying so hard to forget.

Part of me was angry with myself, for allowing another human to destroy me. I had always been stronger than that, sassy and stubborn. But then again, he was not just any human. Several times throughout life he had been my best friend, and he had been the love of my life since I was 15 years old. I had loved my husband, sure, but never like I had loved Jack.

There's just something about that first young love. He had always been the one person I had trusted so completely to never hurt me... or leave me. After all, he had made the promise to always be there for me (even as only a good friend), when he vowed never to lose contact with me again. And he had smashed that promise to pieces, with an over-six-year absence.

So, I guess I shouldn't be surprised at the gray in my hair, the lines and darkness around my eyes, or the apprehensive feeling in my soul. That kind of pain, that sort of injury to your heart, affects the essence of your core and leaves a mark. It becomes a scar, hidden from the eyes of others, deep inside the soul, yet all who truly know you can see it through your eyes. Its lasting effect serves as a reminder to the bearer to be more cautious in the future, with the people they choose to allot that sort of control to. I had vowed that I would fight my heart from ever giving Jack that much power, again.

My therapist had speculated with me that she thought I might have handled Jack's abrupt exit better, if I had sought treatment after my husband, Brad, died. It had never even occurred to me then. I had been focused on our children, making sure that they were grieving in a healthy way, and that their lives suffered as little additional shake-up, or damage, as possible. We had stayed in North Carolina, even though my first instinct had been to return with them to the support of my family in Arkansas. Brad's parents, who were naturally devastated by the loss of their son, and only child, had promised to meet every need of support I might have, if I would please keep his children where they could see them regularly; they didn't feel like they could afford to leave with me. They had gone above and beyond on that promise over the last eight years, always treating me more like their daughter than an in-law. Brad would have been proud of them.

I found my children a spectacular grief counselor, but I never considered that I wasn't handling my own grief the way I should. Therefore, I never had my own wounds treated. I just masterfully covered them up and managed to keep them hidden, even from myself. So, a couple of years later, when this connection with the original love of my life had been severed, the wounds had reopened, and I had been overtaken by a double dose of abandonment issues and grief.

The deeper I fell into despair, the more and more my friends and family had grown concerned, rarely leaving me alone, encouraging me to get help; counseling, meds, anything. I finally surrendered to their wishes, when death had become such a comforting thought. I loved my babies too much to put them through the loss of another parent.

Even after going into counseling and taking meds for depression, it had still taken months before I really started to open the vault where my feelings had been sealed, so many years before. I was a master at controlling, and hiding, my internal demons. And with decades of practice, it had become as involuntary to me as breathing.

My therapist tried multiple methods to uncover the pain and hurt that I had buried so incredibly deep, so I could finally face and deal with it. The first method had cracked the door a little, and I found it intriguing because it used music, which has always had a huge impact on my life and remained a vital factor of my everyday world. I wore headphones, closed my eyes, and the music alternated from ear to ear, which somehow relaxed a portion of my mind, allowing me to recall memories that I had suppressed, so very long ago. This method also had vibrating pads that could be used, instead of the headphones. I held one in each hand and the vibrations would switch from side to side. How it worked to crack my subconscious, I still have no idea, but it was some pretty cool voodoo.

When my progress had plateaued using this method, she presented me with an opportunity that I jumped on, Equine Therapy. I had never heard of such a thing! I had always loved horses and was truly excited to have the opportunity to spend time with them. It was amazing! I worked with different horses from session to session and quickly learned that if I identified a certain horse as behaving like me… assigning my role to them, then it meant I had to figure out who I then became, in our encounter. That really opened my eyes to how I had let other people interact with me and treat me. My favorite horse quickly became Athena. She was a beautiful brown-haired girl, with just a bit of gray coming in here and there. She sported black markings from hoof to knee, that I referred to as her hooker boots. She was sassy and confident. I liked that, it reminded me of the "old" me.

In one session, they placed me and my favorite girl in a corral that was a lot like solitary confinement. It had board walls higher than our heads and only a board's width gap about head-high where you could see out. I had immediately identified Athena as being me, trapped in North Carolina (for the sake of my children), when she kept peering through the gap, to keep an eye on her colt in a nearby pasture. The horse trainer was always present with my therapist at these sessions. When I expressed that Athena hated being kept here, she had encouraged me to open the gate and let Athena leave if she wanted to. She had assured me that Athena would stay close and had never gone off the thousands of times that she'd been allowed to roam. I nervously followed instructions, but as Athena followed me to the door, I looked back at our spectators.

"This is gonna bite y'all in the butt."

As my beautiful girl strolled out of detention, she immediately began eating grass, and the trainer called out to me. "See... she's okay!"

But I wasn't okay. My heart was racing, thinking of how horribly trapped and alone I felt. They claim, and I fully believe, that horses can sense your feelings, which is why this therapy works. And for that very reason, I never took my eyes off her, as she slowly kept munching and easing further and further away from my side. My anxiety increasing with each of her steps, until I was completely uncomfortable with the vast distance between us. I called for her to come back to me. She lifted her head, looked me in the eye... and then bolted toward the front of the ranch.

The three of us panicked immediately and began running for the barn to get some sweet feed and a golf cart to chase after her in. As we sped towards the front, the trainer radioed her ranch hands to confirm that the main gate was closed, so at least Athena couldn't escape the ranch.

The trainer said, surprised, "I can't believe she did this!! But I know where she's going. She used to be in the front pasture, with Rose and Red, so she's probably going to see them."

I had to point out the obvious, since we were dealing with my homesick issue today. "So, you're saying that she's running back to Arkansas to see her friends and family?"

Both the trainer's and my therapist's eyes grew wide with acknowledgement, as they turned to look at me.

I just smirked and said, "Yeah, that's what I thought."

After a few more eye-opening sessions, Athena and her friends had successfully helped me grasp my sanity again. Once I had successfully been able to coach my sweet girl to walk through an obstacle pile of crap that I had built, knee-high and four feet long, to symbolize the emotional junk that had piled up in my soul. Her trainer had whispered to my therapist that Athena would never walk through, or over it. We had proved her wrong again and she acknowledged the accomplishment with, "Well, I'll be damned."

Athena had also reminded me that I had to give stuff to God, and just let it go. The ranch was a Christian facility and had three crosses planted in the center of the property under some beautiful mature oak trees. On this day, after my awesome girl had come across my heap of emotional "baggage," my therapist instructed me to choose an object from the pile. I picked the small orange traffic cone, then Athena led me out of the corral and down the path, eventually, to the crosses. I looked at her and she looked deliberately into my eyes, and I swear she gave a slight nod. I took the cone over to the center cross and set it down, as a symbol that I was leaving all my baggage with God and moving on. Athena then went over and peed on the cone, her way of emphasizing that it was worthless garbage. We all laughed, as Athena walked back nodding her head big-time. True story. Therapy from a horse saved my life.

I could not imagine what I might be like, in this moment, with Jack here now, if I hadn't gotten myself mentally healthy again. Even healthy, I was still struggling with my emotions regarding his return. Thankfully, I had learned to acknowledge signs of struggle as they came on and not to suppress them, the way I had my entire life. My therapist knew all about Jack. There had been hours and hours spent dealing with Jack and my choices and blah, blah, blah. It had been easier dealing with Brad's death than with Jack's history and eventual abandonment.

Naturally, Brad sort of had a pass, as he hadn't actively planned to leave me. My feelings of abandonment with him were completely irrational I realize, but it didn't make them any less present in my subconscious. I had repeatedly told myself, *The man died. I'm sure he was pissed about it too… Let it go, already!* I had finally been able to do so after all those years, and to my surprise, fairly easily. Brad was forgiven and excused. Jack, not so much. And now he was back, asking for another chance. He would need to write a nice thank you note and send a bonus check to my therapist, if he got through this night, without me delivering a strategic, deliberate throat punch to him.

I had never allowed myself to believe that this day would actually come, regardless of how many times I wished and prayed for it. In my mind, I already had my happily ever after with Brad. It was just that it all ended tragically and way too soon. Even though, when it began, I had seen myself as settling. It had turned out that my years with Brad and my memories of him were good, so very, very good. I was beyond thankful for that; I had been extremely blessed.

But things changed six years ago, when Jack confessed that his feelings for me were indeed the same as mine for him. I had wrongly assumed, since our high school breakup, that I was alone in my hang-up issue. Ever since the truth of Jack's feelings for me were introduced into my knowledge base, there would be no way possible for me to ever move on again. No matter how good my life with another man had turned out to be, being able to see the whole picture now, changed things. I was no longer the naïve girl I once was. I had certainty on this issue, because the few times over the last six years that I tried to move on, my heart simply would not get on board with the idea. Settling for someone else was unthinkable. I would never settle again.

2

SETTLING

It was early October during my freshman year at college, and I really wasn't in the mood for a party. But my roommate, whom I was so un-fond of, that I don't even remember her name now, had begged me to go with her. BEGGED ME, a perfect example of one of the many reasons that I didn't particularly care for her. She was a spoiled, whiny, self-absorbed, prissy-type girl; the exact opposite of myself. She had then promptly ditched me upon our arrival. It was crowded, Salt-N-Pepa were pushin' it loud, and the level of drunkenness was increasing by the minute, as most of the attendees were under age and only recently let off their parental leashes. Just like me. However, I had broken rules throughout most of high school and had drank more Boone's Farm Strawberry Hill, Purple Passion and Peppermint Schnapps than I cared to remember; so, control, when it came to alcohol, was not a problem for me, in this chapter of my life. Unlike the other freshmen in the room, this wasn't my first time out of my cage. As I sipped on my red plastic cup of trashcan punch, I surveyed the room and identified those that would be tossing their cookies in the immediate future. I considered telling them to drink the peppermint stuff, 'cause it tasted the same coming up, as it did going down, and left your breath minty fresh.

Good times. Glad those lessons were behind me.

I decided to leave and had just tossed what was left of my punch, and the cup, in the trash. As I turned towards the door, this guy approached me holding two cups, one full of punch, and he was smiling shyly at me. He held out the full cup towards me.

"You're not leaving, are you?"

He was really cute. He had dark brown hair, huge chocolate-brown eyes, was about six-foot-tall, thin but not skinny, and had a smile that lit up the room. I had already noticed him earlier. We had made eye contact at one point across the room, as he was being introduced by another good-looking guy that was being approached by a constant flow of girls wanting hugs, while making inquiries about his friend. He was smiling and shaking hands more than a politician at a rally. He and his friend looked so much alike, I had decided that they must be brothers, but it turned out that they were cousins, by their twin moms.

I accepted the cup as he added, "I hope that you're not, because I just bought you this gift. I hope you like the color, it was all that they had."

"Well, if they made you buy a free drink, then you need to talk to the manager because you've been screwed... That line doesn't really work for you, I hope, 'cause it's pretty lame." His eyes flashed, as his smile grew bigger with his approval of my sass.

"I don't know, it's the first time I've used it... did it work?"

I shook my head minutely with a crooked smirk. He took a sip from his cup, but his eyes never left mine. I held my "gift" but I did not drink it. He extended his right hand and introduced himself.

"I'm Brad…" I let his hand wait for a moment before I gave him mine, while sharing a fake name.

"I'm Chloe."

Shortly after that, my alias was blown when my favorite roommate approached, calling me by my real name, and asking to be introduced to my "hot friend." He had looked down at me in amused shock, then introduced himself to whatshername before looking back at me, with that grin of being impressed, again. I rolled my eyes and smiled back, with my "busted" smirk. After being all but ignored by Brad after their introduction, whatsherface got the message and wandered off back into the herd. We talked for the next couple of hours, never mentioning my fib, until I expressed that it was time that I really needed to be going. He had taken great pleasure in using my real name, with emphasis, when he asked if he could be permitted to escort me home. We had both laughed, as I accepted.

The following Tuesday, I was taken by surprise when a huge bouquet of flowers was delivered. There seemed to be one of every kind of known flower represented. He later confessed, that not knowing my favorite, he was trying to cover all his bases. I had given him my number when he took me home, but only after waiting for him to ask for it (Ladies, always make a man ASK to have more contact with you. Don't just offer yourself up, like you have nothing better to do!). He hadn't even called yet, so I had assumed that when I didn't fall into bed with him, he had tossed it; therefore, I was completely blindsided by the thoughtful gesture. His first call came that evening, to "check to see if I had gotten his flowers." I had given him a hard time, expressing my disappointment in his call not being solely to hear my sweet voice. He had quickly regrouped, and added that of course, that was the REAL reason for the call, it was just that he didn't want to appear addicted to me so quickly; but went on to explain how that was precisely how he was feeling. And he hoped that I would consent to a real date soon, so that he could put an end to the agony that he had discovered, in being so far away from something he had found himself hopelessly attached to, so quickly. Apparently, he had not been able to get me off his mind since we parted.

SWOON

I had learned at the party that he was not a student at the University of Central Arkansas and was only in town visiting, for a family reunion that weekend. He would be returning Sunday to the University of Arkansas in Fayetteville, where he was also a freshman. He was geared toward international relations and wanted to pursue a career as a consultant for the military. All of which sounded incredibly boring to me. I was 18 years old and had absolutely NO idea what I wanted to do when I grew up. So... I was currently an undeclared major and seemed to have a knack for missing class, not studying and failing most of my courses. However, I did currently have an "A" in tennis class. Learning by experience that kids who aren't ready to go to college, really shouldn't go, and should discover who they are and what their goal in life is, before making that step. (I had later gone to technical school and became a dental assistant.)

Brad was everything that I was not. We were in complete balance together. It was easy to be with him, and he had quickly decided that I was all he ever wanted in a woman, and he had bent over backwards to keep me with him. His concentrated efforts were completely silly, as I had no one else interested... I had nowhere else to go, so keeping me wasn't exactly a struggle. Jack and I had lost touch, as I had left immediately after graduation to start the first summer semester at college, and I had no reason to suspect that I ever even crossed his mind, even though he crossed mine, constantly. After all, if he had wanted to be with me, wouldn't he have just said so? I had to let that go and try to make grown-up decisions now. Brad made that easy. Someone good-looking, who adored me, that

THE PARTS I REMEMBER

made me laugh often; I was smitten, and I could live with that.

I consented to a real date, and he had returned to Conway the very next weekend and that had been all it took. We had dated, somehow making the long-distance thing work, all throughout him being in Fayetteville. And I received flowers every Tuesday after each visit; daisies mixed with roses as he now knew that daisies were my favorite, and roses, because there was an "unwritten dating law" which required roses, he had explained. I had dropped out of school after a few semesters at UCA and had moved back home to Little Rock, got a job and worked for minimum wage until the dental assisting thing sounded like something I could get into and enjoy. I liked the medical field but wanted to have "normal" shifts and hours. A dentist's office pretty much assured that. I started technical school with a newfound love for studying and being a straight A student. My social life consisted of two weekends per month. Every so often, I would visit "The Hill" (Fayetteville), and usually my trips were made during football season for home games, but for the most part, every two weeks Brad would come to Little Rock, to spend the weekend with me. It was a four-hour drive, one-way, that included the winding and steep "Pig Trail" which was Highway 23, and the main route anyone used to get from Central to Northwest Arkansas at the time. You had to want to see someone bad to commit to that haul on a regular basis, for over three years.

I saw Jack once, early during Brad's sophomore year, as he was only days from getting married. The encounter had left me crushed and heartbroken, leaving me with no option but to continue on my path with Brad, into a future I thought I could be okay settling into. Brad had become my best friend, someone I enjoyed being with, and in the best way I was capable of, I did love him. Jack was gone forever, and it was time to grow up and move on, for real. It had been easier said than done, but I had managed to do it; at least I had been able to convince my mind that I had achieved closure. My heart had just buried its feelings deep within my core, hopefully to never be heard from again. The following months had passed quickly. I was caught up in the routine of school, work, home, and Brad; I had eagerly accepted it as my normal.

The pivotal weekend occurred during the fall of his junior year. The Razorbacks had a bye week, and Brad asked me if I would like to go camping. We had never gone away together, so this was to be an interesting experiment to see if we really got along as well as we seemed to, or if 24/7 contact would wear on our nerves. I loved being outdoors, so I had eagerly agreed. We decided to save time and meet in the middle, instead of him coming all the way into Little Rock to get me. I was done with classes at the technical college by noon on Fridays, which would give me time to go by my apartment and load up, then head to Morrilton where I would stop and do our grocery shopping, so that by the time Brad arrived, we were ready to pitch camp and get our weekend started. These being the days before cell phones, we had made our best guess at what time we were to meet at the check-in office at Petite Jean State Park. I was glad to see Brad already there, when I pulled into the lot. He had sprung from his car the moment he saw mine and was opening my door before I had the car in park. He was always so thrilled to see me. And seeing his face lit up like a child's, always made mine light up, too. Almost like the way hearing someone laugh hard, makes you laugh. His joy always infected me immediately.

"There's my girl!!" he exclaimed, with a hint of relief in his voice, as I turned off the engine and got out.

"Hey, babe... you're early!" I responded, as he wrapped me up in my bi-weekly bear hug.

"I ditched my last class. I just couldn't wait to see you!"

"YOU should have done the groceries then!!"

"Yeah, I thought about that, but there was no way to reach you. I tried to call before I left, but you weren't home. Are you ready to get checked in?"

"Yep!" He took my hand as he kissed my forehead.

SWOON

As we approached the desk, the ranger greeted us, and Brad gave her his name, as he had called and reserved a spot. He had been very thoughtful and had requested to be near the bath house, so I wouldn't have to walk far to pee. His previous girlfriends must have had pea-size bladders, mine happened to be the size of Alaska. This was one of the many things I was sure that he would learn about me, over this weekend. He paid for the site and then we looked around the little store a few minutes, before we bought some firewood and headed back out to our vehicles. The ranger said that we were welcome to leave one car there, so we unloaded mine into Brad's, as he had all the camping gear strategically crammed into the back of his blue 1983 Cherokee. God love him, he loved his Jeep, but I thought it was the ugliest thing ever. It was a two-door and looked like a giant breadbox. I had never had the heart to tell him.

Our spot was very nice, as tent sites go; it had lots of shade and was perfectly level. We parked and started unloading the gear. I pulled out the sleeping bags and noticed that one still had a tag on it and was much thicker than the other one.

"Is this one new?"

"Yeah, I picked it up for you. I wanted to make sure you would be warm enough.

It's rated to something crazy for cold weather." He had made sure I was close to a bathroom and bought me a heavy-duty sleeping bag.

SWOON

He seemed to sincerely enjoy taking care of me. "Thank you. That was very thoughtful of you." I looked into his eyes and smiled appreciatively.

"I would never forgive myself if you got sick from being out here."

SWOON

"I'll do my best to stay healthy, then," I teased.

After we got the tent up and our things arranged inside, we got started on building our fire. Brad was a pro. He had a blaze going as quick as my dad would have, and I was impressed. I set out the chips and condiments for our planned hot dogs, while he found two sticks and sharpened them with his pocket knife. When he finished, he offered one to me and I took it, as I held the open package of hot dogs out to him, so he could load his own stick. We quickly learned that we preferred our dogs the same way; lightly charred and blistering. We sat close by the fire, with the bag of chips between us as we ate our dogs.

"I would ask you if you want another one, but knowing how you eat, you wouldn't have room for dessert." He had made himself two hot dogs and had finished them both in the time it had taken me to eat only one.

"Dessert? I didn't bring dessert... other than I have some Little Debbies..."

"You didn't think I'd bring my favorite girl on this romantic outing and not bring her chocolate, did you?"

His face was lit up with mischief, as he jumped up and jogged over to the Jeep. He returned with a bag containing graham crackers, marshmallows, and Hershey's bars.

"Can't go camping without s'mores."

SWOON

"I'm allergic to marshmallows." His eyes got HUGE and his mouth fell open.

"I'm so sorry!! I didn't..."

"KIDDING!!" His face changed to immediate relief, then he jumped on me and pushed me backwards, pinning me to the ground.

"You little rat!! I shouldn't let you have one, now! What am I gonna do with you?" Our faces were close enough for him to kiss me, but he just stared into my eyes, as if he were searching for an answer there. Both of us were breathing hard from laughing and the garlicky smell of hot dog breath filled the space between us. He leaned down the extra half inch and rubbed noses with me, before kissing the tip of mine.

SWOON

He pulled back again slightly, and said, "I love you..." for the very first time.

And for the first time since we had started dating, I was able to confirm without a doubt within myself that, "I love you, too..."

I had never seen him so elated! His smile was ear to ear and his eyes were reflecting the fire and sparkling like moonlight on water.

"YES!!" he said in a raised voice, but not quite a holler, as he pressed his body down on mine and then rolled, so that I was on top of him as he kissed me long and good. I must have done a decent job kissing him back, as I felt a third party arise between us and decided I needed to get the reins pulled in.

I raised my head, crossing my arms on his chest, and asked, "So where's my chocolate, or were you just talking big?"

He laughed out loud and slid me off to the side of him, so he could sit up. He reached inside the bag and began loading our sticks with marshmallows. The euphoric smile didn't leave his face the entire weekend, even when I made him sleep in his own sleeping bag.

We hiked to the waterfall on Saturday and made pancakes before packing up on Sunday. He had won me over. He would never have 100% of my heart, but he now had all that was available for me to give. He had called me his girl for a long time, and for the first time, I really felt like I was. My "Plan B" was coming together, and I was going to be okay.

Brad had always voiced his feelings on having to leave me at the end of every visit. Usually during Sunday mornings, at some point, he would start to touch me more and cling physically, saying things like, "These weekends always go by too fast," "I wish you could come back with me," and my favorite... "I could transfer to UALR..." I would have to be tough and firm in my responses, as I tried to encourage him that it was only a few short days before we would be together again, and I was sure that he could manage. Then I'd pull out my sass and tease that I had stuff to do and I couldn't babysit him; he needed to put on his big boy pants and get them headed north. But this time... I didn't want him to go. Well, I had never WANTED him to leave, however, his having to go back had never really bothered me, either. This time, I was actually dreading our goodbye. Two weeks seemed like an eternity! Is this how he had felt all these other visits? Oh, my goodness... this was horrible! I even had to fight tears, when we kissed goodbye, leaving the mountain. After his passionate goodbye kiss, he had again kissed my forehead, but had paused and taken in a deep breath to smell my hair... then spoke sweetly with his lips lightly brushing at my hairline.

"You be good, I love you."

Then he gave me one last big squeeze and turned to get in his Jeep. I walked in a daze to get into my car.

SWOON

As I started the car, Don Henley was on the radio, singing "The Last Worthless Evening." I hoped Don was right, and that my broken heart was being mended. It felt good to have that infatuated feeling again, for the first time in years. I decided not to overthink it, just take each day as it came, and enjoy the ride, for as long as it lasted.

3

SETTLING IN

That fall was the first year we spent our holidays together. Brad had joined my family for lunch on Thanksgiving, then we rolled into his parents' house just in time for dinner. It had been his parents' turn to host the huge family event. I was so nervous. I had met a few of his extended family, but not all of them. He was very close to his aunt, his mom's twin, as the two families had spent a lot of time together when the kids were growing up. Much the way I had envisioned my future family being wrapped in my brother's, one day. Cousins are a very big deal in the south. We view them more as bonus brothers and sisters, really. I had the same huge extended family bond that Brad did, which was good. People who don't come from close families sometimes have a hard time understanding their role in being a part of one, when they marry into them. His family had immediately squashed all my fears and insecurities, treating me as if I had always been around.

We had barely gotten past Thanksgiving, when Brad was back for his extended Christmas break. I was beyond looking forward to having him home for more than just a few days. We had barely let the other one out of our sight. He even stayed most of the time at my apartment, much to my daddy's disapproval. I had sworn and promised him that Brad was sleeping on the couch, but he had just raised an eyebrow at me and said, "MMMMHMMM." Crazy part was... it was the truth! Even with Brad giving me his best pouty face every night, I had managed to sound serious when I would suggest, "You can always go and sleep at your momma's..." He would respond immediately by enthusiastically fluffing his pillow then quickly lying down, covering up, closing his eyes and pretending to start snoring. Or, if we had been making out, he would go take a cold shower after I said good night.

I had tried to keep the reins fairly tight on the "heavy petting" as I knew it was not very nice to allow it, with my mind firmly set on us not going all the way, anytime soon. Occasionally, it had gotten out of hand and gone so far that even I was trying to talk me into it. It had grown progressively less restrained throughout the next spring, basically meaning we were both mostly naked by the time I'd get a hold on my raging hormones and put my foot down, insisting we stop. He had never gotten angry or impatient with me... and a few times, out of guilt, I had used other methods allowing him to release his "tension." Those occasional endings were like little surprises that I liked to spring on him without any warning. I didn't want him to get used to the practice, it was messy.

Splitting Christmas worked out much easier than Thanksgiving had. My family traditionally opened gifts Christmas Eve and his had always opened theirs on Christmas Day. We were thankful for not having to dart between houses and to be able to fully enjoy our time with each family. I discovered later that my family was shocked and disappointed that I had not received an engagement ring as a gift. I was completely surprised by their let-down, as I had not even considered a proposal as a possibility.

My momma had said, "Baby girl, you know it's coming… you've been together over two years!" *We have?* I thought to myself. *Oh, my word, we have!* Time had flown by, I felt as if I had accepted his cup of trashcan punch last week. Two years… sweet crap.

On New Year's Eve, he took me out for an expensive, quiet dinner for two. Then he had driven me out to my parents' house. He drove around the house and back to the barn. He got a duffle bag from the trunk and handed it to me with the explanation of, "You probably want to change out of your good clothes and get into something more comfortable."

"When did you pack this?"

"While you were in the shower a couple of days ago."

"Sneaky." He kissed my forehead and pointed me towards the barn to go change.

When I returned, he had changed into casual clothes too and was sitting on a four-wheeler waiting on me.

"What are you up to?"

"Nothing really, just didn't want to share you with a crowd of loud drunk strangers tonight, so I planned something more our style, to welcome in the New Year. Hop on, beautiful."

I stepped up and threw my leg over the back, sliding on behind him. He hit the starter and we drove out into the pasture. Not far, but just enough that my nose was frozen from the short drive. We pulled up to a newly erected fire pit with a fire built, just waiting to be lit, blankets, and a cooler that I soon learned held champagne, waiting for midnight. He had even remembered to get the cheap little plastic champagne glasses that the bottoms pop off, for effect. He got me settled on a blanket, wrapped up in another one, then he lit the fire. He turned and looked back at me as the fire roared to life.

"Is this going to be okay? I hope you're not disappointed… We can still go out, if you want."

"NO!! This is perfect! And amazing, I might add… You never fail to surprise me." Butterflies suddenly started kicking in my stomach, as my momma's prediction was replaying in my mind: "You know it's coming." Was this it? Was he planning to propose to me tonight? I was regretting eating so much of that expensive meal because suddenly I felt like I might lose it any moment. I guess he noticed the color drain from my face, and he hurried to sit beside me and put his arm around me.

"You okay, sweetheart? You look sick!"

I squirmed to make room between us and opened the blanket I was wrapped in, so he could join me inside of it.

"I'm okay… I think I ate too much. Just hold me for a few minutes and maybe we could lie back?"

"Nope, I'm taking you to the house."

"NO!! Really, I'll be fine in just a few minutes. I'm just overfull, I promise!!"

"Okay, we'll give it a few minutes, but if you're not feeling better quickly, I'm taking you to your mom."

"Deal." I snuggled into his chest as he lay back. I hadn't even noticed the pillow earlier. His head landed on it, and I readjusted mine on his shoulder. He gently stroked my back to comfort me. I lay there trying to concentrate on slowing down my breathing, as I was on the verge of hyperventilating. But my thoughts were still running wild. What would my answer be, if he did ask me to marry him? Was I ready for that? I had become crazy about this man, but was he my forever guy? Feeling me tense slightly at that silent question, he moved his hand to my head and stroked my hair to help soothe me.

"Is something bothering my girl?"

"Not really… I'm just not looking forward to you going back to Fayetteville next week."

"Yeah, me either. But spring break will be here before we know it… Is there anything you would like to plan to do?"

"What did you have in mind?" A different line of questioning was helping me to calm down. I just needed to focus on something else. If this other question was "popped" later, I'd just have to handle it then; thinking about it was making me dizzy.

"I would love to hit Panama City Beach. Think you could get away?"

"Sure! That sounds like exactly what we need! To completely get away from everything, I love it!"

"We have a plan then. I'll get it all booked when I get back to school." He pulled back from me just enough to see my face. "Oh good, your color is back in your face… feeling better?"

"Yes, I'm okay." He pulled me back in close to him and we watched the fire mostly in silence, just holding each other. Occasionally he would inhale deeply with his nose pressed into my hair. And he kissed the top of my head several times. He checked his watch in time for us to get the champagne ready for the big moment. During the quiet, I had prepared myself as best I could for the possibility of the proposal. I realized that I hadn't thought much about Jack in the last few months. I wondered if he was okay and hoped sincerely that he was happy. I reminded myself again that I had not been Jack's forever choice, and that at this point, he probably didn't care a damn thing about me. I needed to do what was best for me. I deserved to be happy, too. I decided that if Brad asked, I would accept. I could be happy with him, I had no doubt of that. Midnight arrived, and we toasted "us" then kissed. We kissed some more as we finished the bottle. The fire died out and we loaded up and drove back to the barn. He never spoke a word of marriage. Feeling so relieved as we pulled up at my apartment, I had to question why, then, did I also feel disappointed? Interesting. After we got inside, I asked him for something that I had never asked of him before.

"I still feel kind of weird. Would you mind sleeping with me tonight? I don't like to be alone when I don't feel good."

"They say that there are no stupid questions, but that, baby, is a **stupid** question!

YES, I will sleep with you!"

"And hold me all night... Spoon maybe?"

"Whatever it takes, I'm your man!" he answered, as he beat his fist on his chest, which made me giggle.

Yeah, I could be happy with this man... He was a good, good man. I discovered that I love being held, while I drift off to sleep. He never slept on the couch again.

Spring break arrived sooner than it felt like it should have. I had finished my technical training and had started working, letting my new employer know, in the interview, that I had plans to be away for spring break. Brad rolled in Friday evening, and we planned to head out early the next morning for the beach. We had dinner with his parents, as we had to be there to pack his summer clothes for the trip. I had never spent much time in his actual bedroom, so as he packed, I did the normal nosy girlfriend digging around. I looked through his high school yearbooks and read aloud the pledges of various girls to stay in touch and of their love for him. He would just roll his eyes and share with me exactly what had been "wrong" with each of them. He was completely unconcerned, as I looked through his desk drawers, and even the ones in his bedside table. I found nothing disturbing or suspicious.

"Where are all of your deep, dark secrets hidden?"

"What do you mean?"

"You know, the box of memorabilia from the one that got away..."

"I won't have one, unless you leave me."

"What?? You had girlfriends in high school... surely!"

"I did, and don't call me Shirley." I looked at him and stuck my tongue out at him.

"Then where's all the evidence, man? The little, black book cough it up!!"

He chuckled to himself lightly.

"I threw it all away... I didn't see any reason to keep it anymore."

"When did you do that?"

"The Sunday afternoon before I went back to school, after our first real date."

"NO WAY! Stop trying to get brownie points, for real, when did you get rid of it?"

"Cross my heart. I knew you were the one I wanted to be with, and I came in from playing the field, that weekend."

I couldn't believe what I was hearing. I knew he had been devoted to me the last year or so, but early on, I had always assumed he was going out with girls on the weekends that we weren't together. I had never asked, because I really didn't want to think about it too much.

We hadn't really had any kind of "understanding" until the end of his sophomore year. Deep down though, I wasn't really surprised. There was something about the way he had always looked at me. Kind of the way my daddy looked at me from time to time, different yet the same; that unconditional look of adoration. Tears welled up in my eyes.

"Why are you crying?" He dropped the clothes in his hand into the suitcase and came and knelt in front of me, sitting on the bed. His eyes searched mine desperately, for what he had said wrong.

"You're too good to me. I don't deserve you."

"Don't be silly, sweetheart. I know it took you longer to fall for me, and that's okay... **I** have you **now,** and that's all that matters to me."

My heart actually missed a beat, as I acknowledged that HE KNEW. Maybe not all the details and the dirty secrets, but he knew that he wasn't the first man to hold my heart. He put his hand under my chin and lifted my face up to look at him.

"If you ever asked me to let you go, I would. I love you too much to see you unhappy. And I truly think that I make you happy. But if someone else is ever what you see as the better deal... it would destroy me to do it... but I would let you go."

"I feel the same way about you. In fact, I'm positive that there are a huge number of girls out there who would be better for you than me..."

"Negative." He wiped my cheeks and gave me his perfect, warm smile as he stood up and asked, "So.... do I need to keep packing?"

"Of course, you goofball!!" He bent over and kissed my forehead.

"No more crazy talk of other women."

"K," I said with a weak smile, then I sat quietly and watched him finish packing.

The next morning, we pulled out before dawn, headed for the white sandy beaches of the Gulf Coast. It turned out that we both loved road trips! We loaded up on junk food and played our favorite music. The fourteen-hour drive flew by, and we were pulling up to our hotel, bouncing with excitement, in what felt like no time at all. The sun was in the process of setting, so we locked up the Jeep and ran to watch, from the beach. As soon as it was dark we returned to get checked in and got our stuff unloaded. We both admitted that we were exhausted and decided to call it a night and get an early start the next morning.

After a relaxing shower, I put my jammies on and crawled into the bed closest to the balcony. Brad had been stretched out, watching TV on the other bed. He shut it off as he got up, kissed my forehead, then grabbed his bathroom gear and went for his turn in the shower. I was fighting to stay awake when he returned, sexy as hell wearing only athletic shorts. He started pulling back the covers on the other bed.

"What the hell do you think you're doing?"

"I promised your dad that there were two beds in the room…"

"Did you promise to sleep in the other one?"

"Well… No, actually."

"Then you had better get your ass over here and hold me! You've lost your natural mind!" He laughed at my reprimand and returned the covers back to their original position, before turning and sliding in beside me. I turned my back to him, as he turned the lamp out and then wrapped his arms around me, pulling me as tight against him as was possible.

"Better?"

"Much, thank you."

He nuzzled my hair with his nose then whispered in my ear, "I love you, sweet dreams, beautiful."

"I love you too."

We were both out immediately and woke the next morning in the exact same position, and spot, when the sun broke the horizon and lit the sky with a full palette of colors.

The week flew by, and before we knew it, we were on the reverse course headed home. We had spent our days on the beach, and our russet-colored skin was the evidence. Our evenings had been spent having fresh seafood for dinner, followed by drinking and dancing at various hot spots with live bands. Surprisingly, we had not been carded once! Back then, I took it as a compliment that I looked older, now I would give my right arm to get carded. I had again braced myself (and had my hopes up, too) for him to propose. It didn't happen, and in my analysis during my first shift to drive, I decided that my momma must be mistaken in what she thought she was reading in his intentions. I glanced over at him, asleep in the passenger's seat, as perfect and beautiful as I'd ever seen him. And the pang of disappointment hit me in the chest. I looked back to the road and shook my head to chase the feeling away. I again reminded myself that I was in no hurry to be someone's ball and chain, anyway. And for all I knew, he had some crazy plan not to marry before he was 30. We had a good thing going, and I was content and happy. Why would I wish for anything to change? In that moment, I forbid myself to ever predict a proposal in the future.

4

SETTLING DOWN

The summer before his senior year arrived, and Brad came home for the duration, just as he had all the previous years. He pretty much stayed with me, spending time with friends and his parents, while I was at work. He came to take me to lunch at least three times a week. We had a great summer, with weekend camping trips to the lake and family gatherings. On his last Saturday in town before heading back for the start of the fall semester, he had asked to take me on a picnic to Pinnacle Mountain. It was one of our frequent outings together as we enjoyed hiking, and the view from the top of the mountain never failed at being breathtaking. He had packed up all my favorite junk foods and even surprised me with my favorite sandwich; peanut butter and banana with a little honey drizzle. Brad had suggested that we wait to hike up the mountain until just before sunset, and we chose the easy trail up the mountain, so we could take our time, talk, and enjoy nature. As promised, the view that evening was spectacular. We reached the summit just as the sun was beginning to go down, creating vivid, bright colors across the sky.

"It's just so perfect and beautiful," I commented as I turned away to take in more of the horizon, putting my back to him.

"Yes, you are... which is why I've got this idea."

His voice had... moved... had he sat down? I turned to discover him down on one knee, holding out a solitaire diamond ring; with a huge diamond, I might add. I must admit, for the first time in my life, I was speechless. My eyes were wide with surprise, and my mouth was hanging open.

"I was smitten with you at first sight and fell in love the first moment I heard your sass, a few minutes later. You are smart, beautiful, funny, driven, and loving... I could name a hundred more qualities that make me want to spend the rest of my life with you; if you need to hear them... Will you marry me... please?"

This was happening... My mind went completely blank, and then only for a moment, Jack's face blurred my vision. I quickly reminded myself that he didn't feel the same way about me and had chosen someone else. It was my turn to be happy. So, very softly, with my voice breaking, as tears filled my eyes in acknowledgement of the death of that dream, I spoke only the word "yes" in a pitiful whimper.

Brad had slipped the ring on my finger and had practically carried me down the mountain in his excitement and relief at my acceptance. Upon returning to my apartment, he followed me inside, but wasn't staying. His mom had made him promise to spend his last night at home, and I'm sure she was waiting on pins and needles for a report. He had kissed me like he may never see me again, then left, giddy as a school boy. I was okay that he hadn't been able to stay. I cried all night long, as I released all of my lingering hope for a future with Jack; then nailed shut the part of my heart and soul that he would forever hold.

Life went back into routine when school started again the next week, and we immediately began planning a big wedding. He was an only child, and I was the only girl in my family, so our parents were going all out. I was surprised that I was enjoying all the attention and the hoopla. I have always relished planning things, so I loved thinking of the smallest details, then seeing them attended to. I was excited to dress shop and to look pretty as a princess, when we found the right one. Tasting cakes, choosing flowers, and planning the after party had all been going really smoothly, and I was happy in the chaos.

And then out of nowhere… Jack called. He was in town for a meeting and wanted to know if we could have dinner. My heart swelled, and I felt as if it would burst, just upon hearing his voice. I reprimanded myself and reminded my heart that we had been friends a long time, and this was just a simple dinner of two friends catching up. I wanted to see him… there was no way I was saying no. He picked me up, and immediately I could tell something was bothering him, but he was hiding it as best he could. Dinner was to be "a surprise" when I asked where we were going. He pulled into O'Donnell's, which I recalled immediately had been the site of our first date.

After we were seated, we visited the memory of our date there. I relayed to him my surprise that he had remembered. We were too young to drive, so it was a double date with his parents; who had sat at a different table, allowing us to have some privacy. We rode home in the back seat, holding hands, with my head resting on his shoulder. Feeling nostalgic, I ordered the same thing I had ordered then. We made small talk and caught up over dinner. He shared that he was surprised and thrilled to discover that I had kept the same number that I had for the phone in my room during high school. He dialed it expecting someone to say he had the wrong number. As we talked more, he seemed taken aback at the news of my upcoming wedding. He admitted that he had been so happy to see my face, that he had not noticed the ring on my hand, nor had he even heard from anyone that I was planning on getting married. He seemed frazzled, as he tried to express his hopes of me being very happy in my future. His smile seemed wounded to me though, pained. I finally couldn't stand the awkwardness any longer.

"What's wrong? You're not okay... and don't try to lie to me, I know you too well."

He looked at me, wide-eyed, took a deep breath then immediately dropped his brave face and opened up that he was, in no way, happy. His marriage was beyond the seventh realm of hell. They already had a child, and he was doing his best to stay, to be a good dad.

My heart broke completely in two. He was supposed to be happy and with the woman of his dreams... It became obvious that he had come here, to me, hoping to find a chance. And I'm ashamed to admit, had he been divorced, he probably would have found one. I would have called off everything, given the ring back, and never had a single doubt about the decision. But he wasn't divorced, not even separated... and I couldn't live with the appearance that I had been a homewrecker, even if it was far from the truth. People would always think that I had been the cause. And there was also his baby to consider. No way was I luring someone's daddy away from their everyday life. I had listened intently, comforting and encouraging him, when I felt I could do so without him seeing through me. If he was leaving her, he would have to do it all on his own, without any nudging from me.

With my not giving him any sign of encouragement that I would be interested in a future with him, he never pressed the conversation in that direction. He had assumed, as I had, with his situation the last time we had met, that I was very happy and was moving into my happily ever after. And he was right. However, my love for him would forever trump any other feeling in my body, he had NOT assumed that, and for that, I was glad. When we pulled back up at my apartment, Journey's "Who's Crying Now" was playing softly in the background. He came around to open my door and had hugged me tight and long when I got out. As we backed away from each other, he had looked into my eyes, almost pleading with me, to say I wanted him to stay with me. I had thanked him for dinner, wished him well, and standing on my tiptoes had kissed him on the cheek before walking away. I loved that man with every fiber of my being, but in that moment, I loved his child more than I loved myself.

Walking away had been the hardest thing I had ever done. I cried myself to sleep again, that night. This was the final time I ever allowed myself to grieve over Jack while I was with Brad. He had never tried to reach me again. He returned home, resolute that he had no other option but to fulfill his commitment. We saw each other, along with our spouses, a few years later, when our class had its ten-year reunion. He'd seemed "off" to me. I noted that they never touched each other, not even something as innocent or easy as holding hands. It seemed strange to me. Brad had been constantly at my side with his arm around me, or holding my hand, and had tried to be an active and interested contributor to any conversation we were a party to. He had worked the room and made a big impression on all my dearest friends... all but one. I could never find the words to describe the way Jack had looked at Brad that evening. It wasn't angry or hateful... just really, really, sad.

Brad graduated in May, and we were married in early June before the immense southern heat became an additional and unwelcomed guest to the wedding. Every detail had gone off without a hitch. The church had been decorated beautifully, and my daddy had managed to give me away without messing up or crying... almost as if he WANTED to give me away. He had laughed when I shared that evaluation with him at the reception. He then explained that my momma had threatened him with bodily harm, if he goofed up my big day.

The reception had been joy-filled, with the large room loud with conversation and laughter; and a cake the size of Texas. We were Baptist, so the REAL party was to be at Brad's parents' country club later that evening. We had a formal dinner there, with an open bar and dancing, after. I had been so focused on everything being perfect that I could look back and say that Jack had not entered my mind the whole day. Sadly, however, I couldn't look on it with mushy love feelings, either. To be real, I'd have to admit that outside of Brad having a role in the events of the day, I really hadn't given him much thought, either. That's how most big weddings go down. You don't even get to enjoy being together during the entire day... Until the wedding night, of course, when the clothes come off.

I think I've been pretty clear in the fact that we had messed around plenty and seen each other naked, countless times during our courtship... I just hadn't allowed full-out intercourse until we were married. Mainly for two reasons that I had never shared, or even admitted to myself. One being I had been very hurt after my previous intimate encounter with Jack. And two, deep down, I had always felt like I was cheating on Jack, and I just couldn't make myself do it. Crazy?? Yeah, pretty much. But, now, I was someone's wife. Brad would be the only person I would ever be cheating on, from this day forward, not that it would ever happen. It just wasn't in my moral fiber. He was my heart now, end of discussion.

Our expensive hotel suite was all done up with rose petals, champagne, and candles, the whole romantic shebang. We were staying here two nights, until our flight to Miami left on Monday. From there we would cruise the Caribbean for a week. I had insisted on us keeping on our full garb the entire day. Did I mention that I looked like a princess in the damn dress? Yeah, I was gorgeous, the dress had cost more than my first car, and I was keeping the friggin' thing on until the last toast was made, and all the glasses were empty. It had taken three grown women to dress me, and bless his heart, I had never considered Brad being left alone, to figure out how to get me out of it.

We had fallen immediately into heavy kissing, the moment we were alone in the room. We were young, in love, drunk, had a hotel room, and did I mention that I looked like a princess? I pushed Brad's tux coat off immediately, and he had gone after his tie as the coat had hit the floor. While I worked on undoing the buttons on his shirt, he managed to remove my veil without ripping half my hair out with it. How, I had no idea. The number of bobby pins on my head had hit triple digits, I was certain. He tossed it to the side, and it had landed perfectly on top of one of the headboard posts on the bed. I pushed his shirt off his shoulders and let it fall to the floor with his coat, wrapping my arms around his neck and knotting my fingers in his thick hair. He pulled me tight against him and went to work on the back of my dress... after several minutes with no progress, he whispered in my ear.

"Did this thing come with tools, or something, to get it off?"

I started giggling... as I remembered, "Yes, yes, it did... oh, CRAP!"

There had indeed been a tool to assist with pulling the loops of the bodice over the twenty tiny satin buttons, starting from the top of my butt to just beneath my shoulder blades. We started laughing and went to our luggage hoping to score something that would work... even if it was scissors. Our luggage had been brought to the hotel earlier during the day, by our families. We had packed two days ago and taken the bags to each of our representatives. To my knowledge, my brother had delivered my luggage to the hotel early that morning.

Toiletry bags, sadly, turned up nothing of use, unless I had married MacGyver. Brad was handy, but I was pretty sure he couldn't make a cutting tool out of floss and tweezers. We had opened every bag, even those that were supposed to go straight to the plane untouched, searching. We crawled from the floor, both barefooted, but I was still fully gowned, and Brad only wore his tux pants. We sat on the bed, trying to decide what to do. Brad tilted his head as he looked past me to the head of the bed.

"What's this?" he asked, as he reached up and grabbed a small box from up between the pillows.

"I hope it's a chainsaw," I answered, full of sass. The note on top was in my momma's handwriting and said simply, "Love, Mom."

Brad took the lid off and his face lit up, when he proclaimed, "It IS a chainsaw!!" He removed the dress tool from the box and spun it around on his pinky. His eyes twinkled as he said soft and deeply, "Come here and turn around." I cocked my head and gave him an "excuse me?" glare.

He started laughing again, and his tone changed to that of an innocent child, with, "Pretty please??" In two minutes, the dress was un-looped, off, and in a heap of tulle and lace on the floor... as were the aforementioned tux pants.

We fell fast and hard onto the king-size bed. Even though we had seen each other naked, hundreds of times, somehow, this time seemed fresh. He suddenly looked different to me, less like a boy and more like a man. The title of "husband" had given him a new confident air. The kissing, touching, and squeezing all played out to the same point where I had insisted that we stop, time and time again in the past, only this time, there would be no such request. When that moment arrived, he paused, looking deeply into my eyes.

He softly kissed my forehead and the tip of my nose, then said teasingly, "I'm sorry, I'm just so used to stopping here, I'm not sure that I know what to do next."

I laughed and shook my head in disbelief, replying, "I do." As I slid my hands down his back, I grabbed his ass firmly and pulled him inside of me.

He gasped, as the feeling of my warmth surrounded him. Then his lips brushed against my ear as he responded, "Such a smart girl, I like the way you think."

Then he proceeded to kiss my neck below my ear and fall into a gentle rhythm with me. Since it had been years since either of us had fully done the deed, it didn't take long, and surprisingly, we arrived at our destination at the same time, in perfect harmony. I can't lie, it was good, as God intended it to be… and the first of five times that occurred throughout our first night together as husband and wife.

I woke around noon, with him spooned up behind me, kissing my bare shoulder. He whispered, "Good afternoon, Mrs. Cooper. I hope you slept well, I sure did… I've drawn a bath for you in our massive tub and ordered some brunch, including mimosas."

And BOOM! At that moment, the rest of what was available of my heart, fell in love with that man. I rolled over to face him, realizing then that I was lying on a bed infested with bobby-pins. We rubbed noses before I snuggled my head onto his bare chest… he was back in nothing but the tux pants, which was sexy as hell, lying on top of the covers. My voice was raspy from sleep and all the talking I had done the day before, when I answered.

"Is there room for two?"

I could hear the smile in his voice when he answered, "I was hoping you would ask that, yes, there is. Let's get you in, and then I'll bring the food when it gets here, and I'll join you. We'll have breakfast in bubbles."

I kissed his chest and softly agreed, "K."

He tugged the sheet I was wrapped in loose from the foot of the bed, then scooped me up, sheet and all, and carried me into the huge bathroom. He made sure I was steady as he released me down to stand.

He was ready to help unwrap me, when I confessed meekly, "I need to pee…"

He motioned grandly toward the separate little room that housed the toilet and bidet.

"I'm not using THAT thing!" I exclaimed, as I walked away like a geisha in her mermaid dress.

He laughed and replied, "I used it this morning. It works pretty well, as far as getting the food stuck between your teeth loose."

I snapped my head back to look at him, just as I realized he was kidding. I laughed so hard that I snorted. I did love his quick wit.

When I reentered the main bath area, the size reminded me of the one in Pretty Woman, especially with the tub in the center of the room. Brad took the sheet from me, holding my hand for balance, as I stepped over into the hot water. He made the connection, when I began to sing Prince's "Kiss" in my best impersonation of Julia Roberts.

He smiled ear to ear, and said, "I just love you…" as he kissed the top of my head. Then he pulled back and removed three more bobby pins and held them up to me proudly, like a hunter with his trophy, as he sat on the edge of the tub.

"Awesome, just seven hundred more to go," I replied.

He chuckled and got up to answer the knock on the door.

"Food's here, Mrs. Cooper."

I hollered back at him "STOP CALLING ME THAT, I KEEP THINKING YOUR MOM IS HERE!"

He responded with a comical, "YES, DEAR." And then he laughed at himself all the way to the door, after I called out, "SMART-ASS!"

It had been just like that, from that day on. We were like peanut butter and jelly, peas and carrots… we just flowed well and belonged together, like two streams coming together and becoming a river.

5

CONTENTMENT

Before graduation, Brad had already accepted a job in North Carolina with a company that contracted in consulting for the military, in every area you can imagine. Areas I had never even thought of. This job meant that we would both be leaving our families, to start our life together in North Carolina. When they had flown us both out for his interview during spring break, we decided if he was hired, that we would try to settle in the southern part of the state, to hopefully avoid some of the unavoidable winter weather and to place ourselves closer to Florida, where we planned to spend a lot of our vacations. Sure, we would have beaches all along the east coast, but we both loved the white, powder-like sand on the gulf in the Florida Panhandle. And after our honeymoon cruise, we hoped to be able to bolt straight down I-95 to Port Canaveral or Miami, to cruise as often as possible; we loved it.

We got settled into our first apartment in Fayetteville, and Brad started his new job on the first of July. Brad thought it was funny that we had moved almost a thousand miles, and he still lived in Fayetteville. I started looking for a job but immediately realized that I was going to hate how much he had to travel. He had no real office in the area but traveled frequently to each one of the nine military bases in the state, for one reason or another, be it meetings, or site visits for things I was never allowed to know about. The words "It's classified" had become dirty words in our home, and I loved throwing them back at him in response to simple questions like "what's for dinner?" and "how was your day?" to the point that he just expected it to be my answer, but he would ask them anyway. I loved the days that he got to work from home. And it worked out, that just like in the civilian world, his work slowed down around major holidays, so that was always nice. And the money didn't suck; I worked to keep busy, not from need. But I was lonely when he was away, so I wanted to work. And I worked full time for well over a year... right up until the ultrasound tech had said, "You knew you were having twins, right?" Brad had almost fainted. And I resigned from my job only a month later.

We immediately started looking for a house. We were going to need more room; a LOT more room. We were both in shock. It was silly that we were completely blindsided by this news because Brad's mom was a twin. I had learned that the night we met; how could we have not anticipated the possibility? We were right in the middle of our second year of marriage, and things were about to change quickly, from what our normal had become. I wanted our babies to grow up like I had, close enough to the city not to be country, but far enough out not to be city. We soon settled on staying in Fayetteville, but in a suburb called Hope Mills. We found a great neighborhood and the sweetest two-story Craftsman-style, four-bedroom home, after looking only a short time. Brad said later that he was sold the minute he saw my face light up, when we pulled into the driveway. It looked like a fairy-tale cottage to me. I had loved it immediately and voiced that I hoped the inside worked for us, because this was home, even if it didn't have a functioning bathroom. As luck would have it, the house had three; all working! I was thrilled that two bedrooms were upstairs, and two, including the master, were downstairs. My vision was that the guest room downstairs would serve as the nursery, until the babies were old enough to move to their own rooms upstairs. We got all moved in and settled, just in time to find out what color the nursery should be. And the answer was pink.

Brad's parents came in for a visit to help with getting the nursery ready and insisted that as their gift for the girls, they wanted to buy all the furniture for the room. Brad and his dad looked like human bottles of pink stomach relief medicine, when his mom and I returned from picking out the furniture. They had been painting all day and were covered in the four shades of pink being used in the room. We had laughed at them, and I had ended up with a pink nose, in the exchange. When the room was done and both cribs in place, it was beautiful and off-the-charts girlie with its frilly curtains, eyelet lace bumper pads, and fairies dangling from the mobiles. All quite opposite of the type of girl their momma was, but for some reason, I felt compelled by some internal force to really frill it up.

We were ready to welcome our sweet girls and were getting nervous about becoming parents. We made a joke about Brad's parents staying as backup, over dinner one evening near the end of their visit. The two had looked at each other as if a light bulb had gone off.

Brad's dad looked at his mom and asked, "Why don't we?"

His mom had smiled, then looked to Brad and me and asked, "Would you really want us to?"

She looked as excited as a kid at Christmas. Brad's dad was retiring on June first, and his mom worked in retail at the mall, just to keep from being bored. It all just clicked and made perfect sense. With the best-laid plans, they would be living here, too, when the babies arrived. Thank

God I adored his parents, or this would have really stunk. Everything came together, and the original Mr. and Mrs. Cooper were in their new home in Arran Hills, another suburb of Fayetteville, for about a week before my first contraction.

Our girls arrived a few weeks ahead of schedule, which was expected, as I was completely out of room for them to grow, and all three of us were becoming miserably uncomfortable with each passing day. Thankfully, Brad was working at Ft. Bragg in Fayetteville on the 29th of June, when I had to make the call in the middle of the afternoon that it was definitely time for him to come home. He arrived so fast that I questioned if he had parachuted out of a C-17, stolen from the base.

"Don't be silly!! The Navy was so excited at the news that they sent an F-14 from Norfolk to get me here."

His eyes were on fire with excitement, until he witnessed me having a contraction, then that fire was immediately replaced with panic and worry as he watched the immense pain flood over me, seriously, the man completely plotzed. He stood in horror, as I worked through the next couple of minutes with only minimal screaming and profanity. Well, in comparison to what the next few hours held, it had been minimal. Brad had later commented that I had used words that he had only heard soldiers use. Don't be misled, I had my favorite swear words, but I tried to keep my daily vocabulary on the classy side.

After I knew Brad was on his way, I had immediately called his parents, and they would be arriving any minute. The plan was for them to drive us, so Brad could focus on me, during the drive. His mom ended up being my labor buddy in the car, as Brad rode shotgun, white as a sheet and about to vomit. We pulled up at the hospital, and as he was opening his door, his dad grabbed his arm.

"Hey, son," Brad looked back at him, and as they locked eyes, he finished, "GAME ON."

It was like he had flipped a switch in Brad's mind. Brad got out of the car and helped me out with a complete look of control and authority that I had never seen before. He never left my side and handled the delivery like a dad having his fourth kid. He was only concerned about my pain level, as I had refused to get an epidural, and making sure that anything else available, to help me in any way be more comfortable was being done.

Olivia Grace had arrived first, and like the Bible story of Esau and Jacob, Claire Elizabeth's right hand emerged wrapped around Livie's left ankle. Three and a half minutes later, Claire had her first cry. And to this day, I swear it was simply because she heard her sister crying, and it upset her. Brad kissed my forehead and told me how very proud he was of me.

Exhausted and out of breath, I panted out, "Are they okay??... Go make sure they're okay, please. I can't see them."

He kissed my forehead again and went to the girls' side, never again taking his eyes off them... mesmerized. After they were wiped down, had scored well on their Apgars and were papoosed up, Brad returned to me with one on each arm. He was still staring down into their perfect, beautiful faces, smiling at them in complete love and devotion. I knew the look well, as it was the exact way he always looked at me.

"Ladies... meet your mommy."

I reached up and took Claire, resting her on my left side, and then he placed Olivia onto my right side. At that moment, my life, my own happiness, was no longer a priority. I was a mom, and my life belonged to them. I would now be devoted to their happiness and well-being.

At the time, you think your life is going to be in a constant stage of exhaustion, filled with poop and crying for the rest of your days. But in reality, it goes by so fast. Before we knew it, we were moving our preschoolers upstairs, each professing the desire to have their own room "like a big girl." We took them to choose their theme for décor, and they got to pick out their bedding and curtains. Then the painting began. Brad's dad came to assist, again, and it was all finished in record time, including the bathroom. We had also given the girls charge of their bathroom accessories, as the upstairs now belonged to them. Brad's parents brought over a cake his mom had made at the café that looked like a twin bed, and we had a grand "moving day" party, complete with a ribbon-cutting ceremony at the base of the stairs. We had all tucked them in that night, each in her own room. I had cried, Brad had laughed at me. And, thus began my "legs and ass training program" as multiple trips up and down the stairs were made daily and doubling at bedtime; more specifically AFTER bedtime. My ass had never looked better, according to Brad.

The time had come, to decide if our family was complete. I knew that Brad loved his girls, but deep down, would love to have a son. We decided to give getting a boy a go and in no time, I was pregnant. The first trimester was much the same as it had been with the girls, a LOT of vomiting and wanting to vomit more. We had an ultrasound at week 18, and we saw, that indeed, we had a boy on board. Brad was beyond ecstatic; cloud nine wasn't high enough. But, in week 19, something went horribly wrong.

It was just like any other day. I had dropped the girls off at preschool and went to the grocery store to pick up some fresh produce for dinner. I was walking across the parking lot back to my SUV, and suddenly, this unbearable sharp pain hit me and wouldn't fade. I managed to get in the truck and reclined the seat, trying not to pass out from the pain. I called Brad, as he was working from home that day, and he headed to come get me. As we hung up, a rush of blood left my body onto the seat, and I called 911. I told them where I was. I remembered seeing the ambulance pull into the parking lot, and I had hit the alarm button, so my truck would guide them to me. At that point, I must have passed out, as I had no other memories until I woke up in recovery.

I had barely opened my eyes and found Brad sitting next to the bed, holding my hand, stroking my hair, and staring at me with a frightened, pained look that I had never seen before. His eyes were red, an obvious sign that he had been crying. I had lost our son and was lucky that I hadn't bled to death. The doctor later said if I hadn't called 911 and waited for Brad to arrive first, I probably wouldn't have made it. The placenta had somehow violently detached, causing the pain and the immediate presence of the massive amount of blood. As I listened to Brad explain and reassure me that I was going to be fine, I swear that I physically felt my heart break. I was beyond devastated. He went on to relay that the doctor said it was extremely rare for this to happen before the third trimester. Leave it to me to blow the statistics. I tortured myself for months, trying to figure out what I had done wrong.

I was discharged two days later. I could have stayed another night but being in the hospital just kept it all so fresh, and I needed to put it behind me. I wanted to go home and be with my girls. When Brad got me home, he insisted that I go straight to bed and was strict with how rowdy the girls could be in my presence. He decided that it would be best for his parents to take the girls home with them, at least for the night. Our sweet babies couldn't understand what had happened to their brother, and the questions kept coming. The best we could do was tell them that he had gone to live with Jesus, and that they would see him in Heaven one day; which started the barrage of questions of when they would get to go. Sometimes you just don't have all the answers. We placed our son, Bradley Joshua, in the cemetery near our house. And I buried a part of me there with him.

After six months, I had approached the subject of trying again. Brad totally freaked out. Turns out the horrible experience of the miscarriage had scared him to death.

"I can't go through that again. I thought I had lost you!"

We had never discussed the events that I didn't remember, from that awful day. I had thought, at first, it was because he didn't want to upset me, and in my grief, I was totally cool with that and had never asked any questions or even mentioned the subject. He had even had the driver's seat in my truck completely replaced within a week, due to the blood stain, and then traded the truck before I ever drove it again because every time he looked at it, he saw my "lifeless body being removed from it." Turns out, he had rolled up to see me being pulled from the truck, covered in my own blood, unconscious. Panicked paramedics started pumping him for my history, allergies and current medications, as soon as he had identified himself as my husband. He said I was literally as white as the sheet I was placed on, and he had watched in horror as they had shoved these garden hose-sized needles in both of my arms. They had placed an oxygen mask on my face that had this little bag at the base of it, and he couldn't tell if I was even breathing. He then broke into tears, as he told me how he was yelling my name and his heartbreak when I never responded, and how hopeless he felt as they loaded me up and closed the doors.

He had rushed to lock up the truck and found himself more traumatized by the amount of blood left behind there. Upon seeing my purse and cell phone in the passenger seat, he had quickly grabbed them, before closing the doors. He somehow had enough wits about him that he called his mom and dad to pick up the girls and had managed to drive, following the ambulance to the hospital. However, he added that he had no memory of the trip... just of praying the entire way, that God wouldn't take me from him. He then recalled that he had been mortified when the doors opened again at the hospital, to discover they had a tube in my throat and were now using a bag to breathe for me, as they quickly unloaded me in the ambulance bay. They had barely paused in the ER, and I was in surgery before he had finished checking me in. All the color had drained from his face, as the memory played out real-time in his mind, as he stared off into the distance. He shook off the memory and looked into my eyes, as he wrapped his arms around me.

"I was sure you were gone, and I've never been more scared, or felt more lost, in my life." He pulled me into his chest and kissed the top of my head. "YOU ARE MY WORLD."

He continued with his story, explaining that the moment I had looked at him in recovery, he had made the decision that we would have no more children. Then, I was floored when he confessed that he had even secretly had a vasectomy in the following weeks, while I was recovering and wouldn't notice, to insure it.

"I will not risk your life for the sake of having another child, ever again."

I was shocked and furious that he had gone to such extreme measures without even discussing it with me. But the look of fear that still showed in his eyes and on his face, just from the memories, kept me from getting outwardly angry. He had forfeited any possibility of having a son, because he loved me more than he did that dream. How can anyone be angry with a love like that? From that moment on, we were a fabulous family of four... at least for a few great years more.

We had taken frequent trips to the beach, and the summer the girls turned six we took them to Disney World. Brad had surprised them with the princess makeover and a breakfast one morning with Cinderella. We had taken over a thousand pictures of that trip and had promised the girls that we would go back one day. I made good on that promise six years later and asked Brad's parents to join us. The girls had a blast, but everywhere I looked I could see Brad, and it had been very hard on me, even though I never let my internal struggle surface for the family to see.

The girls had looked at all the pictures from our first trip a hundred times, and they wanted to recreate as many as possible, to show how much they had grown and changed in the time between visits. I noticed that they had no interest in recreating the ones that had included their daddy. And I stopped asking after the third opportunity, when I put two and two together and came up with four. I wasn't the only one sporting a brave face on this trip. I didn't mention it, but it dawned on me that their wanting to return here had nothing to do with the magic and everything to do with feeling a connection to Brad. On the last night of that trip, we were watching the amazing fireworks at Magic Kingdom when I heard Livie whisper to Claire,

"Do ya think that Daddy can see them?"

Claire had simply nodded in response, and the sisters had put their arms around each other and leaned their heads together for the remainder of the show. I looked to Brad's parents' faces, they were still watching the sky, but the tears in their eyes made it obvious that they had heard my sweet girl, too.

With all his scheming and plans for him not to lose me, he had not secured a way for me not to lose *him*; for *us* not to lose him. The memory of that day is one that will never fade enough to satisfy me. He had just run into Fayetteville, for what was to be a quick afternoon meeting at Ft. Bragg. He had promised that he would be home in plenty of time for dinner. Dinner had come and gone, and he hadn't come home. I had tried his cell repeatedly, with no answer, turns out it had been thrown from the car and wasn't found till later. The woman at fault (whose name was Linda), was also killed. She had been applying mascara when she crossed the center line. We know this because she had a huge black smear on her cheek, and the brush was found still gripped in her hand. She hit Brad head on, at 70 miles per hour, as she was also speeding. They said that it all happened so fast that Brad may not have even seen it coming, as they found no evidence of him trying to react... no skid marks, no swerve. They had assured me that he had been killed instantly.

I had friends come over, one to stay with the girls, whom I couldn't bear to tell yet, and another to drive me to Brad's parents. Of course, it was apparent that I was in shock, and his mother had known immediately that her baby was gone, before I even opened my mouth. I had simply nodded my head to confirm the look in her eyes, and she had collapsed, wailing, into Mr. Cooper's arms, behind her.

Life can be a real bitch... all you have to do is take your eyes off of her for one moment. Everything had been so perfect, and in an instant, it was all upside down. For some silly reason, I had held on to, cherished even, the fact that he had kept his last promise to me, he had left in plenty of time to be home for dinner. Robert Burns said it best: "The best-laid schemes (or plans) of mice and men often go awry."

6

SURVIVING

Initially, time seemed to have stopped after Brad was killed. It was all I could do to make it through each day, and each day that came seemed to be longer than the last. However, after about six months, when the initial shock had faded, time seemed to speed up and over-correct itself by flying by. Maybe because as a single mom of two, I was constantly running my ass off. Thankfully, Brad had been a planner and had a crazy amount of life insurance on us both, and I would never have to work again, unless I chose to. I made the decision to continue to be a stay-at-home mom until the girls went away to college, and then I would reevaluate my life's focus and go from there. My babies were eight years old when they lost their dad. They were beautiful, smart little third-graders at that time, who loved gymnastics, dance, and playing dress-up. Being identical twins, they both shared their dad's chestnut-brown hair and insisted on it being longer than shoulder length. They also had his perfect olive skin, but they had managed to get my green eyes. Their growth chart was just beginning to reveal that they would not be as short as I was, either.

How on earth I had managed to birth and continue to raise girlie girls, was a mystery. They were everything I had never been. I had always been a tomboy, apart from being on drill team (now called dance team) in school. I felt like a fish out of water when it came to living in the frilly world. I did my best at figuring out how to swim in the unfamiliar waters, and before long, I could buy matching tights and bows without gagging.

Brad's parents had been a constant, supportive presence, but also very respectful of my role as the parent. His dad had valiantly stepped up to fill in for his son for every Donuts with Dad, Father-Daughter Dance, and countless car wash fundraisers, so that my precious daughters never felt left out or awkward. They had never missed a recital or denied any request from the girls to spend the night with them, eventually reserving an entire weekend every month to spend with them, when their schedules grew more crowded as the girls grew older. His mom had even attended as my support, when it was time to have "the talk."

In middle school, both girls followed their mom's footsteps and made the dance team. I must admit that I loved that there were pom-poms in my world again. AND it meant that I had an excuse to go to football games. Brad would have been proud that I had managed to instill a love for sports in them, too. Their love of football budded from their finding the players cute, and soon they were asking me to explain the game, so they could talk to these guys with some knowledge and not appear "stupid." This also happened to be how I fell in love with the game. I had wanted to attract Jack with my football savvy and asked my brother to teach me every detail, when I started 10th grade. The girls and I now had something in common, outside of their activities. They embraced their family history and became devoted Razorback fans. We even went to games when they played South Carolina, and once we made it a girls' weekend and went to Knoxville for the Tennessee game.

Outside of their dance team abilities, it turned out that they both were amazingly gifted gymnasts. They loved the thrill of competition and had such fierce competitive spirits. They were so good, so young, that we had been approached about gearing them towards an Olympic goal. We had been so excited, but the girls quickly declined when it became clear how much time would be spent away from me. Their closeness with me was not a sacrifice they were willing to make, and I had been so relieved. I would sacrifice anything for them, and if it had become the dream that they wanted to pursue, I would have been all in, supporting them. They were happy to compete at the high school level and hoped to be recruited for college, which I had no doubt would happen and most likely with multiple offers. I just wanted them to be happy. The moment I sensed that they were no longer enjoying themselves, I would shut it down. But for now, we pretty much lived between the high school and the gym.

Claire also loved to sing. Olivia could sing just as well, but being my shy one, she had no desire to share the talent outside of the family. Livie was my bookworm. She loved to learn. Both girls were honor roll students, but Livie could never get enough knowledge. So, while her sister focused on choir, in her free time, Liv was on the debate, trivia, and book bowl teams. Claire had made all-state in ninth and tenth grade with her voice, and Liv had her share of brain trophies. I was proud of my well-rounded girls, even though their schedules kept us on the go almost every night during the week, and at least three Saturdays a month held at least one competition for one, or both, of them. We never sat still it seemed, which made time race by. We were already taking college entrance exams and looking at the schools we thought would be a good fit for them. Thank God they wanted to stay together, if possible, for college; it would make my world so much easier if we could manage that.

Of course, I can't tell you about my wonderful, beautiful girls, without mentioning the never-ending line of boys interested in them. Seriously, if their dad was alive, he would be worn out from being on guard duty. It had only been in recent months that there seemed to be a constant starting to form. Claire had been with her boyfriend, Logan, for four months now, and Liv had an even longer run, going of five months, with Tyler. Both boys were very polite and attentive to my girls, and I approved highly of them both. Nice boys were a welcome change, especially after the ugly scene we had with one of Claire's "bad boy" crushes, early in sophomore year.

Dude shall remain nameless, but I ran into him out to eat with another girl, after he had given my sweet girl some lame excuse as to why he had to break their plans that night. I had introduced myself to his date as his girlfriend's mom and had asked her the question of what she thought of a guy that would cheat on his girlfriend? Her facial expression left me no doubt that she had no idea that he was seeing someone. I then shamed him verbally and left them to discuss it between themselves. I stopped on my way home and picked up Claire's favorite ice cream, chocolate almond, and prepared my heart for the upcoming break of my daughter's. I cued up Carrie Underwood's "Before He Cheats" for the drive. Later, I was shocked to learn that he had the misfortune of not one but TWO flat tires on opposite sides of his car, when he went to leave that night. Thank goodness, no damage to the tires, it was almost as if all the air had just escaped from them both... WEIRD. Claire had given me a knowing smile, as she had relayed the story of the flat tires to me, when she came home from school that Monday.

"Why are you looking at ME like that?"

"I'm just proud that I have a momma with a redneck streak in her." She had hugged me and gone to her room and never cried another tear over that dude again.

Their dad would have approved of their current selections. They seemed to genuinely love spending time at our house, and we spent many evenings fixing big dinners and watching TV or movies, together. They had discovered the girls' and my wicked competitive nature, the first time we had played games together. I discovered that the guys thought I was cool, when Tyler had tried to play matchmaker and set me up with his single dad, after getting to know me. I had found a very delicate way to decline, so not to hurt his feelings. It was a tempting offer, his dad was very good-looking, liked to hunt and go camping. He was honestly right up my alley, if I had wanted to pursue another relationship. But we had settled into a nice routine that the girls were happy with, and I had no desire to change anything, ESPECIALLY involving the "love department." I adored that when we had competitions, the boys wanted to come along to support "their women." Brad would have liked that, too. We were discussing a weekend trip to Myrtle Beach, before school started. The girls couldn't believe that I would even consider letting their boyfriends come away with us overnight. I informed them that they would be sleeping in the same room with me, and I reminded them that I am a very light sleeper. Apparently, the boys were not surprised by this information, as they had been told the story of the flat tires early on in their courtship, by Captain Cheater Pants himself. I think they were actually concerned that I might string them up and gut them like a deer, if they stepped a toe out of line. I just let their thoughts run away with them. A little fear is never a bad thing to have in your favor.

Deep down, I had always known that my precious girls sincerely wanted me to find someone and be happy again. We even had the discussion a few times, when a situation would require that we discuss it, like when Tyler had suggested that he would like for his dad to ask me out. That had actually been the last time we had visited the subject. After the guys had gone home that night, the three of us had gotten into our pajamas, grabbed a tub of ice cream, and cuddled up on the couch with spoons. And for the first time in their lives, I had shared with them the story of Jack. They had been caught completely off guard to learn that there had been... that there still was... another love in my life, besides their dad.

Olivia commented, "That explains why you are so respectful of our relationships and our feelings! Other parents treat their kids' love interest like they expect them to change every week and get worried if it goes on too long with one person. Now I see why you've never pushed us to play the field!! YOU fell in true love in high school!!"

"That I did, baby girl... and hard. No one can predict or control when real, true, forever love will happen, it just happens. Your daddy swore that he fell fully for me the night we met. And I believe that he did. I'm sorry to admit that it took me a bit longer to fall for him because of the spell my heart was already under, but he eventually broke through, and we had a good life together."

"And he became your best friend. I hope I get to marry my best friend," Claire added.

"Me too, sweet girl, me too... But I promise you that I will never tell you that you are too young for your love to be the forever kind. TRUE, it's not probable that your high school romances are the ones... but it IS possible."

They had asked questions about where this "Jack" was now and what my current feelings were for him. I told them everything that had happened and what my suspicions were about his situation. They asked if I had kept anything from that relationship, like mementos and pictures. We ended up crawling up into the attic, to retrieve three boxes that I hadn't seen in years. They contained everything from notes to pom-poms, including my yearbooks and an old men's athletic T-shirt that I set aside and washed, later; then hid it in the back of one of the bottom drawers in my dresser.

"Oh, wow, Mom, he was REALLY cute!!" Claire had exclaimed.

"Yeah… he was. He actually IS still really attractive… well, last time I saw a recent picture of him, he was."

Olivia noted, "He's kind of Daddy's opposite… don't you think?"

"Well, Daddy's hair was MUCH darker, but still brown."

Claire remarked, "But he's SO tall and the eyes… those BLUE, BLUE eyes!!

SWOON!"

"Yes, they were quite the attention-getter." I laughed at their reactions. We had stayed up till the wee hours, looking through the boxes. They were amazed at how "HUGE" my pom-poms were, compared to the pitiful excuse for ones that they used now.

"Didn't your arms get tired?" Liv asked.

"Yes, ma'am."

Claire added, "And these shoes, is this really leather?"

"Yep, we called those rah-rahs."

They both looked at me like I was crazy. Then Liv found a small box. My heart ached the moment that she held it up and began to open it.

"Oh, Momma!! It's a…"

"Charm bracelet," I finished her sentence for her as tears filled my eyes. "Jack gave me that for my sixteenth birthday. I wore it every day, until well after graduation."

"The heart is beautiful!!" Claire commented as she reached over and let the large crystal charm rest in her palm, as Liv was holding the bracelet up.

"I love the elegant script of your monogram, on this one!" Liv added.

"I was told that he had worked his ass off to pay for it, when I was scolded for breaking up with him."

Liv looked to my face, mortified. "WHO SCOLDED YOU??"

"One of his best friends, and I deserved it, he was right."

"Wow…" Claire responded. "He must have had some good friends."

"He did. We both did. High school was a really good time in my life, and that's why I'm trying to make sure that you have the same quality experience."

Livie asked, "Why did you break up with him?"

"It's complicated… but basically, because I was an immature idiot."

They both looked at me, understanding that I really didn't want to talk about it anymore and had let the question go with that vague answer. We wound down after that. Claire had lovingly placed my bracelet back into its box. As they told me that I was the absolute coolest parent ever. I agreed with a "DUH!" They had laughed, kissed me goodnight, and we had all gone to bed. At least, I thought we all had. But when I woke up the next morning, the box with my bracelet was sitting on my nightstand, with a note that read:

*"Momma~ True love never dies.
It just waits for its time."*

I had taken the bracelet out and put it on for only a moment, before it made my heart ache so bad that I was forced to put it back in the box, along with the note, and then placed it in the drawer of the nightstand. However, their note lingered in my heart from that moment on. The deep meaning in them leaving it for me wasn't only that I should never give up on my true love returning, but that they wanted me to love and be loved again. They were cool with me going on with someone other than their daddy. My sweet girls were so mature and had grown up too fast. I was so extremely proud. They never mentioned me dating, the bracelet, or Jack, again. I think they could see that his memory was painful for me.

That discussion seemed to have happened a lifetime ago. But I had no doubt that my girls' stance remained unchanged. They would insist that I go to dinner with Jack. They would be disappointed in me if I were to tell them later that he had come to see me, and I blew him off. It was time to face him and hear him out.

7

AT FIRST SIGHT

I was ready for dinner early, but I had already planned to leave late, HE would wait on ME this time, so I sat down on the couch and watched the remainder of a re-run of "Friends" on TV. Ironically, it was the final episode when Rachel returns to Ross forever. In the past, this episode had always made me cry, but tonight, I just felt numb, with no reaction at all. As they kissed, I turned off the TV and took a deep, calming breath, acknowledging that I had to leave, I could dawdle no more. If only I could make his ass sit and wait for six years to hear from me again (just so he would know how it felt), I'd do it. A small part of me wondered just how long he would wait. He knows me better than most, so he would be ready for my tardiness. Knowing it was my way of throwing a fit, he would think it was cute, making me more endearing. Damn. Confirming his belief that he knew me well, would make him happy, double damn. But being early would show me as eager, same with being on time. It might appear welcoming, even. Well, DAMN again. I do not want him to think this is going to be easy for him. But the

A. B. WOOD

play I had chosen to use, from the ultimate female attitude play book, was certain to be a no-gainer… maybe even the loss of several yards. I had to keep it together.

He had his work cut out for him, if a chance of a life with me was what he was after. There is massive emotional damage to repair that he himself had caused. Tonight, would reveal if he was in possession of the specific emotional tools required to undertake a job of this magnitude. I was determined to be tough and not be an easy sell. But I knew, once those blue eyes met mine, I would forget my own name and possibly even something as simple as how to breathe. I checked the time. It was straight up the time for us to meet—eight o'clock—when I grabbed my purse, threw my phone in it, and went to my truck. I loved to aggravate my younger brother, Will, by calling my SUV a truck. And I almost considered calling him, to help calm my nerves, as I backed out of the garage. But I had decided to wait to share what was going on with him until I was clear on what was actually happening. I was pleased to discover that the rain that had come down all day had finally stopped. The streets were still wet and glistening. I rolled down my window just to feel the cool, damp air in my face, hoping that the fresh air would help clear my head and calm my nerves. I loved the smell of rain. And appreciated how rain always left the world looking clean and smelling renewed.

It could have been a quick ten-minute drive to Belle LaBlues but I took the long way, just to make it twenty. I obeyed all traffic laws and, when no one was behind me, I slowed to five miles per hour under the speed limit. I even stopped for a yellow light that I could have easily made. As I pulled into the restaurant parking lot, twenty-five minutes later, I became aware of the radio for the first time… Cee Lo was singing "Only You," again, ironic. I immediately saw Jack waiting outside. Not trying to call me, or even checking his phone… He was just standing outside the doors, with his hands in his pockets, as if he was there to simply enjoy the evening air. He was also dressed nice, but still casual, in jeans and a tucked-in apricot button-down shirt over a basic white T-shirt. His short brown hair was stylishly spiked. It had been what... almost 19 years since the night we had dinner together? Yet, he still looked as flawless in my eyes as he always did in my dreams. His eyes met mine, as I'm sure had happened with every driver entering the lot for the past 45 minutes, as he surveyed each vehicle, hoping it was mine. Immediately his mouth changed to a cocky half grin, revealing that he was not surprised at my tardiness. Yeah, he was on to me... crap. And now my heart was racing... the after-effect of that damn grin. Not good, I wasn't even parked yet, and I was already losing my composure. I tried to regain my focus, as I blocked the vision of him from returning from my short-term memory and concentrated on maneuvering in the parking lot. But my heart was loose now, and being unrestrained, it raced on.

I pulled into the furthest open space, but even before I had the car in park... he was there, waiting to open my door. Sweet Crap! Had he broken into a full-out sprint when he identified me?

SWOON

STOP IT! I said to myself. I turned my head to look at him, as I slowly shifted into park. The doors automatically unlocked with a loud "clunk," when I shut off the engine. With that noise, my door flew open, and his arms were around me before I could even process what was happening. I was in shock. I raised my forearms, attempting to return the embrace, as they were all I could move. He had me pinned to my seat! I was only able to lightly pat his back in response to his awkward hug. I tried to fight the feeling of total relief that washed over my body with his touch, and I felt immediately intoxicated being surrounded by his scent. I felt as if I were melting. He pulled back, only inches, took my face in his hands, looked into my eyes... and kissed me. The warm feeling permeated through me to the center of my core. After a moment, I found my nerve as my anger and disappointment with him returned to the surface, and I placed both my hands on his chest and forced him back and off of me. The horn blew, as his back hit the steering wheel. He took in my wide-eyed, shocked face, and gave me a crooked grin.

"You can't imagine how good it is to see you," he said.

Then he smiled the ear-to-ear smile that I love more than chocolate or pie or... life. *I'll bet I can imagine*, I thought. If it was relatively half as good as it was for me to see him, it was immense. Relief flushed through every fiber of my being. I could die, right now, and I'd be completely cool with it. But I couldn't let him read that in my eyes, so I looked away, just to break the connection.

"Let's get you out," he said, unfastening my seat belt.

As soon as I was unrestrained, he backed out, stood straight and then he held his hand out for me to take. I shook my head slightly in disbelief, purely for his benefit, as I removed the keys from the ignition, picked up my purse from the passenger's seat, and took his hand. I had forgotten how tall he really was, a full foot taller than me, at least. He closed his hand around mine, and that's when the tingle started. From the tips of my fingers, *ZAP* through my entire body, just as it had so many years ago, each time we held hands as kids. I flashed back to the first time he had taken my hand, when we were in high school.

We had not been a couple long, when I walked out of class to find him waiting in the hall, right outside the door. His face had lit up when I emerged from the classroom.

"Shall we go to lunch?" he asked, as he took my books, adding them to his, holding them all under his arm against his side, and with his free hand he had taken mine.

Our fingers wove together in a perfect fit. I recalled looking up at him and being swept away by his eyes and smile, as always. He had asked me about class, first, and then if I was hungry, as we walked hand in hand, to my locker. He released me long enough for me to put my things away, then eagerly took my hand again and smiled. After stopping at his locker, the exact same occurrence, only this time, he had looked into my eyes as he raised my hand to his lips and sweetly kissed the back of my hand then smiled and said, "Muy bonita." I had been confused, until I remembered he had just left Spanish class.

"Show-off," I responded, as I laughed lightly, but still unable to look away from his adoring gaze. He again interlocked his fingers with mine, and we had walked on, to the cafeteria. I felt 15 again, when I returned to reality.

He had locked my truck and was closing the door, when I came back to my senses. I had to get my game face back on! I gently tried to retrieve my hand, but his grip was firm, and as I had just remembered... he again raised my hand to his lips. This time, he slowly kissed the center of my fingers, and then the back of my hand, closing his eyes and pausing mid second kiss, as if giving thanks for the moment and soaking it in as deeply as possible. The fine hairs on the back of my neck stood up, and the tingle went through my entire body again. *ZAP* *Damn him*, I thought, as I realized he had strategically given me his left hand, as he knew that I would accept his assistance with my right hand, allowing me to twist to exit the vehicle. There was no justifiable reason to let go as we ended up comfortably side by side, allowing us to remain hand in hand, as we walked. Always the gentleman, he finally had to release me to open the restaurant door, allowing me to walk through ahead of him. I took in a deep breath and focused on trying to get my wits back about me.

The host greeted us as we approached, and Jack requested a table for two.

"It'll be just a few minutes," he replied.

As he turned back to face me, Jack extended his arm towards seating available for us to take, while we waited for a table.

As I turned and began to sit, I said, "I'm so late, I'm surprised you waited."

"I knew you would be, to torture and punish me." He winked and flashed a half grin.

"And, just how long were you prepared to wait?"

"Till they closed, then I would have tried again by calling you tomorrow."

All I could manage was a "Hmpff" sound in response, as I rolled my eyes and looked away.

"And in case you were wondering, it would have been my same plan the day after, and the day after that. I'm guessing you knew me well enough to know that I would not go quietly into the night this time, and that's why you decided just to give in and get it over with, up front."

Again, that smile, causing my heart to flutter. I wish he'd put that damn thing away, it was going to be the death of me.

I raised my eyebrows and managed to answer, "Yeah, something like that." I forced myself to look away from him.

The truth was, I wouldn't have been able to think about anything else but him, knowing that he was here. MY need to see him was stronger than any of my body's needs for actual survival at this point. Food, water, shelter?? Nope, nope, NOPE!! All I needed was him. Laying eyes on him met every need I currently had, or could foresee having, for the rest of my natural life. Having officially, personally confirmed that he was alive, well, perfect, and beautiful, had made me complete. Again, I could die now and have not one single complaint.

I excused myself to the ladies' room. I had to get a grip! As I walked slowly away from him, I remembered that my butt had been one of his favorite features of mine, and fortunately, it still looked pretty good after all these years, especially in this particular pair of jeans, so I made sure he had ample time to get a good, long look. I pushed the door open, stepped inside and immediately looked myself over in the mirror. My nerves had my stomach doing somersaults. I truly felt as if I could vomit. What I needed was some cold water on my face. However, that would not be makeup friendly. I tried to take some slow, deep breaths, as I closed my eyes and tried to think of something obscure. For whatever reason, the first thought I had was Santa Claus. Yeah, Santa would work. I felt a giggle come over me. I opened my eyes, washed my hands, and took one more deep breath before giving myself the nod to leave. I felt more centered when I returned to him. He stood as I approached, looking concerned, and waited for me to return to my seat.

As he sat back down, he asked, "Are you okay?"

"Never better, I just needed to wash my hands. You touched them, and I have no idea where you've been." ZING!!! Nice one!! I was proud of me!! I held a cocky smirk on my face and waited for his reply, as I visualized me spiking a ball back to his side of the net.

"Well played," was his only answer, and he returned my cocky smirk with one of his own.

The way he looked at me made me speechless. It was that look of unconditional love and adoration, as if I could never be more perfect in his eyes. It was a look that I hadn't seen directed at me since Brad died, over eight years ago. It was starting to break down my very weak wall, I had to look away, before I gave in and leaned in to kiss him. I was fighting with everything I could muster not to touch him, just to be sure he was real and actually sitting next to me. I still felt like I was dreaming one of my many dreams of us being reunited and was praying I didn't wake any time soon.

We sat quietly for several minutes. I could sense him staring at my face, but I avoided looking at him, busying myself with taking in the décor of the area we were waiting in and people-watching those at the bar, some of whom had obviously been there for far too long. A party of four walked past us towards the door, and only moments later the host addressed us, "Your table is ready, please follow me." Jack stood and offered me his hand again. This time,

I was prepared for the gesture, and I handed him my purse. I could tell he fought back a laugh, then grinning ear to ear, turned to follow the host with my purse hanging, proudly, from his forearm. I found myself checking out his ass as he walked in front of me. Oh yeah... I had always loved that part of him, too. I stood still for a moment, dazed. He quickly glanced back and asked, "You coming?" Shaking my head to clear the fog, I joined in at the rear of the parade to our table.

The host stopped, and he stood with him, until I had taken my seat in the booth that he had motioned to. After I sat down, he handed me my purse and winked at me. Our waitress appeared immediately after the host wished us a good meal and stepped away. She introduced herself, asking the normal polite questions like how we were this evening, and if the rain had stopped, then she gave us her well-rehearsed speech on the specials. It then occurred to me... there was no freakin' way I could eat. My stomach was in a knot, on top of being upside down. The waitress had brought water but asked what else we would like to drink. I needed to calm my nerves and give my stomach a slap, so I ordered my favorite scotch on the rocks. As the words left my mouth his eyes got huge, and he reared his head back with a look of surprise.

"Really!?"

I met his look with raised eyebrows and answered, "Yes... someone drove me to drink," as I gave him my best smart-ass smirk.

"I guess so!"

We both returned our attention to the waitress, who was catching on that this was a somewhat tense meeting to be a party to, more awkward than a first date, even. Her expression was slightly uncomfortable, but she worked to keep her face pleasant, as she turned her attention to him.

"I'll have your best single barrel bourbon, straight up," he told her. *Guess his nerves need settling too*, I thought.

The waitress left to get our drinks, I turned my attention to him and I said, "I'm really not hungry."

He gave me a disapproving look, then returned his eyes to the menu before responding, "If you're so very angry with me after all that I have put you through, the least you can do is stick it to me with a huge tab."

I had to laugh, he had me again, as I had already considered that plan, earlier. His eyes looked like fire, as they lit up at the sound of my laugh. *CRAP! No more laughing!!* I reprimanded myself. *He's so happy to see me, I don't think a fart would even be perceived as unattractive. Dammit.* Then the thought occurred to me... how exactly did he know that he had put me through anything? To my knowledge, he had not utilized any of the many available connections he had through friends, to me, so how had he come by this intelligence? I was about to ask this very question but was distracted when the waitress returned with our drinks and asked if we were ready to order.

I went with the big tab plan. I ordered the 12oz ribeye, rare, and added a lobster tail. And, "YES, I would LOVE to add a salad for just two dollars more! And please do LOAD the baked potato for another two dollars!"

He never flinched, just smiled, and said, "That's my girl. Are you sure you don't want an appetizer as well?"

I responded in the classiest way I could think of and stuck my tongue out at him. He smiled even bigger at me, as a small chuckle escaped. Confusion washed over our waitress' face. She had no idea what she was in the middle of. Were we together, or not? And that was the question of the hour, one we all wanted an answer to. I felt sorry for her as I watched her process the situation, as she tilted her head at him, ready for his order. He asked for a small garden salad with Ranch dressing. Following my considerably larger dinner, the simple request seemed odd. We had ordered opposite as most couples would, but the waitress lingered a moment before she asked him, "Just the salad?" and when he nodded that she was correct, she looked even more confused as she thanked us, took our menus and walked away. I assumed his order was a sign that his stomach was equally as upside down as mine. Or more likely, that he knew that he would be eating most of what I had ordered, just like in high school. As soon as she was away from us, he returned his attention, and a newly inquisitive gaze, to me. *Great*, I thought, *no more interruptions, buckle up... here we go.*

Only then, did I notice that there was music piped into the room. "Against All Odds." Gee thanks, Phil Collins, what did I ever do to you?

8

EXPLANATIONS

"You look amazing."

I slowly met his eyes and held his stare. Finally, I responded, "How's your wife?" and followed the question with a sarcastic, crooked smile. I had intended to say *lovely wife* but seeing how I had always thought she resembled a troll doll, and not in a cute way, I didn't think I could say it with a straight face. I then continued to express my not-so-heartfelt wish for her health.

"She's well, I hope... I'd hate to hear that she had fallen victim to some violent affliction like leprosy or being covered in painful boils."

I had caught him off guard with the question, but a slight chuckle escaped in his exhale, at my suggestion of gross illnesses.

"I wouldn't. But I'll be nice and leave it with... we are recently divorced. And I'd wager on a guess that no tears were shed by either party, having the guarantee in knowing that none were shed, here."

I had to take a moment and let that information sink in. She was gone. Wow! Hard to believe, after all these years, he had finally managed to take his leave from her, as he had desperately wanted to, a large majority of the entire marriage. I deeply wanted details, but I didn't want him to know that I was that interested, or, that having confirmation of him being single was a point in his favor. I would have to let that one go, for now, but I couldn't stop myself from singing "*Ding Dong the Witch is Dead*" in my head, as I decided to go forward in my interrogation.

"So... why are you here? Because if it's to seduce, then completely abandon me, you've already executed that maneuver, over twenty years ago... flawlessly, I might add, so it really doesn't need any work."

As the words left my mouth, my mind went back in time, to the final time we saw each other when we were both still LEGALLY single.

After weeks of letters and phone conversations, he had come to me. Nervous, yet calm, I waited. For the love of my life, I waited. The anticipation of his arms around me warmed me to my soul. I knew that I would feel a level of happiness and completeness that I hadn't felt in years, in the single moment of his arrival. With his knock on my apartment door, my heart leapt. I peeked through the peep hole just to get a first glimpse, but he was looking down. Just seeing the top of his head was enough to send my heart into double time. I opened the door, but kept my body behind it, to hide me from his sight, until it closed again. He entered, looking just as perfect as I remembered, and it brought tears to my eyes. My heart, my joy, my love... was there.

He wasted no time wrapping me in a sincere, tight embrace. Peace immediately swept over me, tears escaped briefly and softly, with the relief of the emotional release I felt. In his arms at last, I was whole again. He was warm, yet my body tingled, as if chilled by his touch. He ran his fingers through my hair as he looked lovingly at me. When he smiled at me, his own relief was obvious in his eyes. He gently placed his mouth on mine, and the feeling was electric. Warmth flooded through my body as I leaned in, never wanting more from life than that moment. I broke the bond, solely from the need to calm my racing heart and catch my breath. Oh, how very much I loved him! How had I never told him this fact years before? How stupid I had been! I stepped away, knowing that he had tasted the wine on my lips, and asked if he cared for a drink.

"I'll have what you're having."

He followed me into the kitchen. As I poured his wine, he stood beside me, looking at me as if he had never seen anything more beautiful, or a more welcome sight. The look was so obvious, he could not hide that he loved me anymore than I could conceal my love for him. Our faces simply screamed it, in silent proclamations.

We returned to the living room and sat close together on the couch. In only a few moments, the desire to be held and to hold, overpowered us. I leaned in, and he wrapped his arms around me, pulling me to his chest. I placed my legs across his lap, and he cradled me, pulling me in to him, even closer. He sighed, contently, and kissed my forehead. We tried to talk small talk, but the passion, the desire, for more would not be denied and could not be contained. The kisses came, soft and warm, wanted... eager. They became more urgent, I wanted him. With everything I was, with all I had, I wanted him. My desire to be so close with him that we would appear as one, was starting to overwhelm me.

As he moved forward to the edge of the couch, we turned to face each other. Fingers knotted in each other's hair, moist lips moving across every inch of the other's face and neck. As I unbuttoned his outer shirt, I could feel the heat radiating off his body, and I swear I could hear his heart beating. Then I realized that it was mine, POUNDING so hard and so fast it might explode... Which would have been fine, to die in this moment would be poetic... perfect. As I undid the next-to-last button, I had to gently tug the rest of the shirt free from his jeans, so I could reach the final one, which enabled me to urgently push this overlaying shirt free from his body. *LAYERS!! UGH!!* Why did it have to be winter? His shirt fell, narrowly missing his glass of wine that he had placed on the floor.

We were perfectly positioned for him to push me back and lie on top of me. Why didn't he do it? I WANTED him to do it! Then I realized there was no room. The couch was small, a loveseat, really, and not at all designed for this type of activity. He was way too tall, and even I, with my short stature, was uncomfortable lying on it, unless I curled up on my side. Suddenly, he stood and asked me to stand with him.

"I want to feel you against me."

I eagerly granted his request, and again we were wrapped in each other's arms. An unbreakable embrace, as we both were pulling ourselves into the other, with the desire to be closer. The kisses were longer now and left me breathless. I had loved the feeling of his hands roaming, like he wanted to touch every inch of me, as if making a mental map of the terrain. His fingers lightly ran up my side from my waist and gently brushed against my right breast on their way to the back of my neck. He cradled my head in his hand and my hair fell between his fingers. His thumb gently stroked my cheekbone as he pulled my head to one side, exposing the opposite side of my neck, so he could kiss it.

I said, "We need to stop, before we get into trouble," meaning we would go too far and end up even more buried in our immoral behavior. We were both in relationships, I had been dating Brad for several months, we hadn't made a commitment, but I was seeing no one else. However, Jack's relationship was VERY committed, as he was scheduled to report to the altar in only a few days. My choice of wording made it sound like we were kids afraid our parents would walk in, which was the memory we both were having… the vision of us, as kids, making out in his parents' living room on the sofa.

Again… "We need to stop before we get into trouble." Nothing slowed, much less stopped. I did not want him to think of me as "easy," either. I gently pushed him back. He relented and, for a moment, looked deep into my eyes before he asked to be excused for a minute. I watched him walk to the bathroom, still dazed and euphoric with passion. I had been thankful for the break, because it gave me a chance to catch my breath and slow my pounding heart.

I picked up my glass of wine, walked into my bedroom and to the other side of the bed to look out of the window, hoping to clear the euphoric fog from my head. Snow was on its way. I love snow, and I was as excited as a small child waiting for the first flake to fall. As I stood at the window, holding the curtains back with my right arm, he was suddenly behind me. His approach had been stealth-like, and by the time I was aware of his return, his arms were wrapped tightly around me, pulling me back against his chest. He pressed his left cheek to my right one; heaven. Feeling his warm breath on my skin, I couldn't resist turning to face him, his embrace relenting only enough to allow me to turn. Then his mouth was on mine again. I gently pushed free after only a moment and motioned my intention to set my glass down on the bedside table. He had held on to my free hand gently.

As soon as I had set it down, I returned to him, with a gentle push towards the bed, as our mouths once again found each other. So much for being good. He followed my lead, and holding me in one arm, had gently supported my weight until our bodies met the mattress. He allowed himself to land beside me on his side, and he immediately began to undo my clothing, starting with the button on my jeans, then slowly, my zipper. Still kissing me passionately, he slid his hand under my panties and began to tenderly, yet firmly, touch me with only a finger. The thrill was more than I could stand, as every pleasure neuron in my body fired at once, and I began to pull upward on his arm in a silent plea for him to stop. As I did so, I thought, *nice bicep*, because I could feel that every muscle in his arm was rigid, revealing very definitive lines, even in his forearm, which all alluded to his strength.

SWOON

He granted my silent request, as his kiss morphed into a brief, sweet grin, as he realized that my plea had been out of pleasure overload, not an actual desire for him to stop. His kisses returned, as he slowly slid his hand up and across my stomach, and upon reaching my side, he pulled us together tightly then rolled... pulling me on top of him.

His voice startled me, calling me back from the memory.

"**OUCH**... Is that **REALLY** how you see our night together? That I baited you into bed and then just walked away with no further thought... no attachment? You **seriously** think that it means nothing to me?"

I continued to glare at him but didn't respond. Truthfully, I wasn't sure if that's how I felt or not, even after years of analyzing it. I seemed to still find myself on the fence. Some days on one side or the other of the issue, but most days I was sitting smack dab on the fence. And the crazy thing was, this was ancient history, over twenty years ago, to be exact. But it was easier to be angry about that encounter than his most recent abandonment (of the last six years), which stemmed only from him trying to keep peace at home.

Deep down, I just wanted to be angry, so I could stay on the "you abandoned me" side of the fence, long enough to become a permanent resident. Then, I would be able to get over him and walk away and not look back. But some days, I found that I still could plant both feet firmly on the understanding/protective side and be happy living there, too. UGH! And I hated that side, because I felt naïve and gullible over there. I firmly held my gaze and tried to bore a hole right through him.

He was still shell-shocked by my accusation, so I went in for the kill.

"And then to surface again, after you just cut me off, like a cancer, six years ago? After a weak good-bye, that didn't even register with me at the time, as being the beginning of a total and complete disconnection? You PROMISED to never leave me again! I lost my mind, thank you very much! I wanted to DIE, because it was easier than trying to breathe every day without you! And you think you can come waltzing in and make up for all of that with 'I love you, let's have dinner'?!" Trying not to cry, I finished my rant with my teeth clenched… "YOU ABANDONED ME!"

As many times as I had worked on and practiced this speech over and over in my head, in the hopes of this day arriving, not once had I anticipated my tone being so hateful and ugly sounding. I guess because it had always played out in my head, never had I verbally released my feelings. I was almost as taken aback by my venom-filled words as he appeared to be. His lips moved into a tight line, his eyes widened, and he half shook his head in confusion as he took a deep breath.

"I hate to hear this… ALL of this. I've been painfully aware that you had suffered, but I never imagined that you thought I had abandoned you! That's not at all what my intentions were, in either case!" He paused, as he was obviously trying to process his thoughts into words, for me. "I knew that you had gone through a rough time, but I had no idea that it had been that severe. The thought of you wanting to die, because of me… I just can't…" he trailed off, shaking his head in disbelief, for a moment. Then his eyes snapped back to mine, as he found his voice again.

"I'm so very sorry… I NEVER would have caused you pain like that—EVER. I was stupid and did what I felt

I had committed myself to do, when I got married. It was against everything my gut was telling me, but I thought it was too late to call it off. I wanted to… desperately! Then six years ago, I completely thought I was protecting you, and I thought you knew that."

My gaze remained unchanged as I replied, "Perhaps making a phone call, or in the least, sending a freakin' email, would have enlightened me to your intentions, or you, to my feelings." I slowly blinked then and rolled my eyes away.

"I fought that urge every… single… day," he said quietly. Believing and wanting the statement to be a lie, I returned my eyes to his, searching for the slightest hint of truth. Unfortunately, his whole face was covered in it. He actually looked as if crying was a possibility. I felt my resolve slip a bit. Crap. I slowly lowered my eyes and stared at the table, giving him a chance to compose himself and regroup.

"Not knowing if you were okay, about drove me crazy. I finally found a way I could, somewhat, keep tabs on you, and that was through Facebook. I checked your wall almost every day. I was so proud of you going back to school and getting your degree. I'm surprised you didn't hear me yell 'that's my girl!!' when I read that you graduated with honors. You looked beautiful with your gold cords. I knew you could do it, great job."

I knew he had added the "great job" to require that I respond; slick. A quiet, "Thank you," was all he got. No eye contact, my gaze never left the table. At least that answered my question on how he had gotten information about how I was. Stupid social media, ugh! Then it occurred to me, he wasn't on Facebook. He had given friends believable excuses for why he had deleted his account, but I had always guessed that she had insisted he close it. One less thing for her to have to police, daily. How exactly was he checking on me "almost every day" using it? So, I asked.

"How, exactly, are you checking my Facebook, daily? You're not on Facebook."

"True, I'm not, but Albert Hawking is. I created him and opened an account, just so I could see you—your picture, I mean. I needed your smile fresh in my mind, to help me endure, as I struggled to continue to play my part in my world every day. Some days, I think it just made the pain worse, but it was a price I've been willing to pay all these years. I was so thrilled to discover I could see posts occasionally."

I made a mental note to check my privacy settings.

"It would make my week when you would make me laugh. I've missed your humor most, I think. But the flip-side, discovering you were sad, or sick, would always hit me like bricks, and I was helpless to make things better, or take care of you, and I had to fight using every fiber of restraint that I had, to keep from calling to check on you."

"So, you've been lurking… stalking me on Facebook. That's creepy."

"Yeah, well… when you're desperate…" His voice trailed off.

"Your desperation developed out of a choice, YOUR choice. I've been right here, Facebook, phone, same damn email address that I KNOW you have engraved on your brain forever, and NOTHING."

OUR email, an address I had created just for him, and him only, to reach me. No one else knew it existed. Not for sneaky reasons, I had no one to hide anything from. It was just a place we could chat, without being interrupted by other contacts that were online at the same time; there were no other contacts there. Like an idiot, I had continued to check it for the last six years, less frequently now than in the first few weeks and months after the separation, but right up until now. Matter of fact, I had just checked it less than a week ago. How pathetic was that? I looked away again, as I felt tears welling in my eyes in reaction to realizing how pitiful I truly was.

"You obviously haven't checked it in the last few hours. You may find more there than you bargained for, next time you log in."

My eyes snapped back up to meet his and found that they were twinkling with mischief and were accompanied by a cocky grin that made him look adorable. What did "more there than I'd bargained for" mean? He didn't even have access to that account, what could possibly be in there so suddenly that could remotely surprise me? What was he up to? He held his gaze firmly on my eyes, in an almost challenging way, as if he dared me to look it up, right then and there. I was more than tempted to grab my phone and check it, just so I could appear unimpressed with whatever he had planted there. I managed to fight off the urge and just returned his glare with a look that said, "Bring it on, Jackass." He only smiled bigger.

Our server was approaching with our salads. She quickly placed them on the table as she said, looking at me, "Your food will be out shortly." Then she turned to him. "Are you sure I can't get anything else for you?"

He politely told her we were fine, she turned and walked away. I realized I had never touched my drink, and my nerves were all but frazzled, now. I immediately picked it up and took a larger than average sip. The scotch burned as it hit my tongue, traveling all the way down till it reached my stomach. Bringing with it an instant soothing that I was becoming in desperate need of.

"I love you," he said. My eyes instinctively snapped up to meet his, out of shock at the sudden declaration, as he continued, "I've never stopped or wavered in that— EVER. Not one single moment since high school, have I not loved you, please HEAR that. Please... KNOW THAT, if you believe nothing else that I say, tonight."

I had to look away. The tears came... HUGE tears, the kind that always bring wailing and snot with them.

"Excuse me," I said. My voice breaking and almost inaudible, I grabbed my purse, scooted out of the booth, and left the table.

Immediately, I had to decide what my intention was, because I had no idea. Where was I going? No clue. I was in self-preservation mode, running on autopilot. I walked back through the seating area, past the hostess desk, and out the doors, before I comprehended that I was leaving. The cool, damp air of an early fall hit me; snapping me into reality, and I froze. What the hell was I doing?? I just walked out on the man I loved! I was losing it! I felt like all my circuits were overloaded, as all my pent-up emotions seemed to fire all at once. Too much information for one night, and we'd been together what... 30 minutes? I started moving again, quickly, to my truck, double time, not quite a full jog (I was in heels, after all) but close. I began frantically pressing the unlock button on my remote, several feet away from my truck, knowing, without a doubt, that he would guess that I had bolted, and he'd be in fast pursuit at any moment. Since his legs were considerably longer than mine, and naturally, he was NOT in heels, he could catch me with little to no effort.

I violently yanked the door open and jumped inside, almost simultaneously starting the engine. I took a quick glance for passing traffic behind me, before I backed out. I was barely clear of my parking space and shifting into drive, when he emerged hurriedly from the building. Our eyes met as I passed. He looked dejected and broken, and his eyes were pleading. I turned my eyes to face the road, as he hung his head and I watched in the rearview mirror, as he turned and went back inside. I put on my seat belt, as I pulled out of the parking lot and turned towards home. "Hard Habit to Break" was on the radio; I pushed the button to change the station from eighties to country, only to find Miranda Lambert singing her heartfelt "Over You." *GEEZ!!* I pushed the next preset and was relieved to find

"Welcome to the Jungle." *Thank God.* I cranked the volume to drown out his voice from my mind.

9

DAM BURST

The drive home was a blur. You know how you zone out and then are amazed and left to wonder how you made it to your destination? That totally happened. As I turned into my neighborhood, the song on the radio brought me back to reality, one of my many favorite Lady Antebellum songs, "All We'd Ever Need." When had I changed the station again? I could not hold the never-ending stream of huge tears back any longer. They flowed hard and fast, along with the aforementioned snot, sexy. It seemed like it took forever for the garage door to get up and out of my way, so I could pull in. Why did I feel the need to own such a big vehicle? If I drove a Miata, I'd be parked and in the house for five minutes, already.

As I pulled my truck into its limited allotted space, tears were now dripping from my jaw bone like a leaky faucet, and I bit my bottom lip to keep from wailing, afraid the neighbors might hear and think I needed help. I shut off the engine, resting my head on the steering wheel as I waited for the garage door to close behind me; my shoulders heaving with my silent sobs. As the door made contact with the ground, I grabbed my purse, got out of the truck, and went inside as quickly as I could, while avoiding all the garage clutter, including the girls' balance beam. As soon as I stepped into the house and closed the door behind me, I screamed at the top of my lungs, threw my purse onto the kitchen counter, and left a trail of clothes all the way to my bedroom, starting with the damn high heels. I grabbed the box of tissues off the dresser and collapsed onto the bed.

Full body sobs, and wailing, FINALLY made their exit. Every ounce of pain, hurt, regret, and disappointment that I had fought to contain for years… decades actually… I let consume me. Every emotion regarding him that I had held at bay all these years, a battle for control I had waged every minute of every day, for as long as I could remember, I finally embraced it, letting it all take over. For hours, I cried full on, all out, hours and hours. Then, finally, as abruptly as it had all started, it was over. It just stopped as suddenly as if a switch had been thrown. I rolled over from my fetal position, onto my back.

The soft glow from my salt lamp was the only light between my bedroom and the kitchen, where the light over the stove was always on, just like my grandparents had always been. Leaving it burning was like an unwritten law in the family. Funny the customs that we choose to hold on to and carry on. They provided just enough light for me to see and regain my bearings. I tried to recall the moments after I arrived home. Where was my purse? *The kitchen counter.* That's right, I remember now. As my thoughts cleared, and I regained my normal rate of breathing, I realized how exhausted I felt. I got up, grabbed my pajamas, and walked into the bathroom. The sight of me in the mirror was disturbing, but over the years I'd grown accustomed to seeing "frazzled me" in reflections, as this wasn't my first breakdown; I had several partial ones on record. I took out my contacts and turned on the cold water, to wash my face. As I splashed the cool water onto my hot cheeks, calm flushed over me. Then I realized what had me so worked up: relief. He still loved me. For years, I had longed to know the answer to that question. I had prayed, begged God, just to give me that answer, and once it was finally delivered, my entire composure had crumbled. The relief had been like a dam bursting. I didn't have to feel like a fool, holding on to a pipe dream, any more. HE STILL LOVED ME. I had been right all along. I put my glasses on, brushed my teeth, then went to my purse, to get my phone.

One missed call and one voicemail, four hours ago. This meant he was concerned, but knew not to push. Four hours… It was one in the morning, it was tomorrow. I had lost my mind for FOUR hours and still felt like it wasn't all out, as if it had simply retreated to regroup, then attack again, when I wouldn't see it coming. I touched the voicemail icon, then his name. I had never removed his contact information from my phone, even after several years had passed. I had tried several times, but I just could not make myself hit "delete." It felt like I was taking a step towards deleting him from my life forever, and that, I could never do, so in my phone, he had remained. I had, however, changed his name to "Jack" in the listing, when it became his new name. I wondered if he had considered this as a possibility, as his call the day before had come through as "unavailable" on my screen. Had he really thought that I wouldn't answer if I knew it was him? Would I have answered? *Of course, you would have. You would have puked first, but you would've answered.* My heart was right. I braced myself to hear, again, the sweetest voice I knew, it never failed to make my heart flutter.

"Hey, it's me… I hope you made it home okay… I'm sorry I upset you; that was the very thing that I did not want to happen. Please just check our email. You know me… I'll be waiting, impatiently, to hear from you, so I hope that happens soon… I love you."

My first instinct was to delete it, but my soul was thrilled, that for the first time EVER in my entire life, I had his voice recorded. It was mine and I could listen to it whenever, wherever, and however many times I wanted to, so, I left it. I exited out to the home screen as I went to my desk, opened my laptop, and pulled up our email. I found a new item in the inbox. And for the first time in six years, three months, and thirteen days (now), it wasn't from Yahoo. I couldn't help but stare at the sender's email address—myjournal4u—letting it soak in. It was dated the day before, only a short time before his call had come through. I opened it to find only a brief message:

> My love,
>
> Please log in to this email, on Yahoo, and make yourself at home there, as it is all my gift to you. My only request is that you please open each and every item you find there, as each contains a piece of my love and devotion to you.
>
> Login: myjournal4u
>
> Password: 4mygirl
>
> All my love, always

My hands were trembling as I opened a new window and began to type. When the account opened, I couldn't believe my eyes, there were over 800 "new" items in the inbox. Just out of curiosity, I checked the sent file. Only the one email I had just read, was there. I clicked back to the inbox, and for whatever reason, my instinct was to open the oldest item first, which it seemed took forever to reach, when I started scrolling down. It was dated over *six* years ago. My heart stopped, and a huge lump rose in my throat, as I clicked to open it. It began as his notes in high school always had, "My Sunshine." Tears filled my eyes again. That was it, BOOM, he had me. Soft target acquired, and a direct hit... BULL'S-EYE! Anytime I had ever been miffed, upset, or out-right angry, his using his chosen pet name for me had always melted away any negative emotion. After taking a slow, deep breath I continued reading.

My Sunshine,

I sit here to write, devastated that my connection with you Has been severed. It's been two weeks since I've had the assurance that you are okay. I hadn't realized how dependent I had become on the comfort of knowing that you were in this world, alive and well, almost every day. I've fallen into near madness, with concern and worry for you, and I miss you more than I feel I can bear.

I can trust no one. She watches my every move; counts every breath of my entire day. I can't begin to relay how I detest her. Why I ever committed my life to her, I have no answer. My children are the only positive that I have from it all. I'm thankful for that. They are my solace and joy. And I will remain here to be with them daily.

I have decided to keep in touch, in a way, with you, here. I hope that one day you will read this and any future ramblings I may need to release from my broken soul. My hope is that here I will be able to feel close to you... connected in some way. I'm afraid without it, I will lose my mind completely.

I want you to know that I love you, truly, madly, deeply, and I think of you often. I hope you are well; HAPPY, with days filled with laughter. And I impatiently wait for the day that we are together again even if it is only to be close friends. I miss you.

My love forever

Tears streamed freely again. I went to the pantry to get another box of tissues. I would need stock in Kleenex to keep up with my usage, at the rate I was on. I opened the box, setting it on the desk, as I sat back down. I closed the entry and opened the next, dated ten days after the first. There was a screenshot of a Facebook post I had made. It had been in the early period of my darkest days. It was scary to read my own words now, knowing how close to ending my life I had come.

"I've never felt more alone, or more desperate and lost, than I do in this moment in my life."

I had been very near suicide, hanging by a thread, and swinging from my very last nerve; all unintended bad puns. He had been my closest friend, and we had sworn, even voiced our commitment, to keep our relationship in that status, as long as he was married.

He was devoted to his children and doing the right thing, regardless of his own happiness. I was, in no way, a threat. I would never have been capable of being a home-wrecker, it just wasn't in my nature. But she had apparently found communication between us that she found to be unacceptable and had thrown a fit. After losing contact with him and being accused of everything you could name, by her, I had shut down my whole world. I ended the only near-serious relationship I had been in since my husband died, which had started at Jack's urging for me to please try and find happiness again. I stopped any social interactions with my friends and rarely even showered. I lost major weight, so all my clothes looked like hand-me-downs.

Thank God I didn't have a job. It had been all I could do to act "normal" when my girls were with me. I'd done a supreme job of keeping them sheltered from my struggle. And my in-laws had kept them often, concerned of any extra stress being a single mom may have been causing. My time with my girls had been the only part of every day that I didn't actively cry; I had forbidden myself to expose my pain to them. As his first entry stated about his children, my girls had also been my solace. Truly, the only thing that had saved my life was my love for them and the desire for them not to have to grow up as orphans. But with my soul being completely torn in two, I was functioning solely from my brainstem. Breathe in. Breathe out. No emotion other than indescribable, unfathomable grief. I was dead inside. He'd written a short response to the screenshot:

I'm devastated, my love. You cannot give into the hopelessness that I'm feeling too. This information has destroyed any hope I had for your well-being. So very worried now, knowing that your pain is as vast as my own. I'm trying to hug your heart with my own. PLEASE FEEL ME!!

As I remembered those days, and so many days since, I recalled how I had thought I was crazy, the many times I had sensed his presence, both in my soul and in my mind. There had been times, I could swear, we had conversations in my head. I could concentrate on him, picturing his facial features as clearly as I could, as I quieted my mind to every thought but him. I'd hear his voice in my head, as clear as if he had been holding me, whispering in my ear. But that had to be lunacy at its height, right? Normal humans don't have this type of superpower. However, when I had shared these episodes with my therapist, she had told me studies had been done and had shown that this type of mental connection was possible, especially with two souls so deeply bonded. That type of devotion carries an energy that only God can explain. This type of telepathy has been written about between twins and other tightly woven human relationships for centuries. I had jokingly begun referring to it as the Luke and Leia curse.

The sound of a "POP" snapped me back into the moment. In the other window, where our email remained open, the message indicator glowed with a "1." It had been over six years since that email account had seen a chat message, so it took a moment for me to register what it meant. My heart began to race as realization hit. *It's almost 2 a.m. and he's up? He's worried about me.* I clicked the tab to open the window. The chat box automatically opened at the bottom of the screen.

> "Hey, I was hoping I'd find you here. I've been waiting and watching for you to be 'active' since I got in. I hope you're okay, and I'm so very sorry if I crossed a line. By the way, your dinner was excellent."

I can't believe he ate my dinner, I thought. He has to be messing with me. So, I replied:

"Really? You ate my dinner? You really are an ass."

"No, not really. You know me better than that. I told the waitress to bring the check, and that I hoped the staff would be permitted to enjoy it. I explained that you weren't feeling well, and that I had lost my appetite."

"I'm not sorry about that."

"That's my girl. So, have you accessed the email account that I gave you? I assume that's why you're here."

I knew that was a wasted question. He knew good and well I was logged onto the other account. If he could see me active here, there was no doubt, that as a contact on the other account, he could see me active there as well, but I played along. I was too tired and emotionally spent to play any games.

"Yeah."

"And?"

I had no words to convey what I was feeling, plus, I had only opened two items, it was a bit early to make a judgement regarding the contents of the entire account. But I did have a pretty good idea of what to expect in the other 800-plus entries. So, I stated the obvious.

"Seems to be a lot there. You've been a very busy boy."

"Yeah, well, you never left my mind, EVER."

"Well, I guess if it proves anything, it would be that. Why didn't you just actually email me?"

"I was paranoid that she would find out, and I, in no way, wanted you attacked by her again, you had done nothing wrong. I also knew the limit of my ability to restrain myself and that I would not be able to leave it as email, which would lead to certain trouble. It was the hardest thing I have ever done, staying away from you, knowing that you were hurting and struggling. You're my best friend."

I was nowhere near ready to start this conversation again; I needed time to process all that I had already been flooded with. I had to shut it down, now, before I became a blubbering mess, again.

"I need to go. I'm very tired and have had a lot to process for one day."

"Alright, Sunshine, I understand. But can I ask one last thing?"

"Doubt I could stop you, so go ahead."

"Will you have dinner with me tonight? Please?"

He had to be kidding. Was he simply trying to make me insane, or was he possibly trying to kill me?

"Good night."

There was a small pause before he replied.

"Sleep well and sweet dreams. 'Nite, my love."

I half slammed the screen down on my laptop. Took a deep breath, grabbed my cell phone and walked back to my bedroom. I crawled into bed, nestled deep down under the covers, and took in another deep, cleansing breath. I stared up at the ceiling fan and slowly exhaled. Thank God today was Saturday, and my girls were with their grandparents until Sunday night. Sixteen-year-old girls had enough drama of their own, without being witnesses to their mother's. And with them away, I could scream out loud again if I needed to… so I did. Thinking of my girls, I couldn't help but wonder what their reaction would be, when they learned that Jack had indeed returned. I lay there with my burning, red, tear-drained eyes still fixed on the ceiling fan, as their sweetly written words, "True love never dies, it just waits for its time," began to mingle and intertwine with his voice: "Not one single moment since high school, have I not loved you."

I suddenly remembered a night after a basketball game, when there had been a fight. Jack and Brett, the guy I had been dating for months, who went to the opposing high school, had locked it up on the parking lot as we left the game. Jack had dominated in the confrontation and had only stopped his flawless assault when I had stepped to the center of the circle of spectators, placing myself between the boys. Jack's eyes had been enraged and unfocused, when I placed my hand on his chest. My touch had caused him to snap out of his trance and look me in the eyes, but he still held his fists ready to throw the next round of punches. "PLEASE STOP!" I begged him, and the next second, a call of warning had been yelled from the crowd that school faculty were on their way; so, I wasn't sure which had actually ended the altercation.

I'd never been told what had initially sparked the incident to happen. After all these years, I could not recall if I had ever asked either of them what had happened during the game that had escalated to that moment on the parking lot. I didn't think I ever had, as I remembered being very angry with Jack for the severe beating he had delivered; I had avoided speaking to him for weeks. I knew Brett was humiliated and would rather I not mention it, so I never did. But with Jack's admission at dinner, it dawned on me that it had to be the root of their initial argument. He had still been in love with me, so his protectiveness, mixed with jealousy, had to have been an easily fueled fire, sparked by my boyfriend, whom I remembered to be a smart-ass when confronted. The realization made me wish that Jack had made me leave with him, that night. I would have, with little to no encouragement. A simple request for my hand, or his arm around me, guiding me away and I would have been at his side. Instead, I'd been left to sneak Brett's shirt past my parents that night, to try to wash the blood out of it before he went home. I don't know how he explained what had happened to his face, to his parents.

It was all obvious to me now. Jack's heart had been broken; my boyfriend getting in his face had been more than he could bear. Hindsight is such a bitter pill to swallow sometimes. I replayed his profession of love from tonight's encounter, over and over again in my mind, until exhaustion finally conquered, and sleep overcame me.

10

ENLIGHTENED

I woke to the sound of my silenced phone buzzing on the nightstand. I picked it up to see if it was my girls, but it was him; so much for him impatiently waiting to hear from me. *Sweet crap, what time was it?* I reached out and turned the clock towards me, squinting to read the display, 10:31. Wow, I had slept, REALLY slept, for over eight hours without being medicated. That was new.

BUZZZZZ-BUZZZZZ-BUZZZZZ

Ignoring him would prove fruitless. I might as well get it over with, so I could get on with my day, in peace. I answered, my voice sounding scratchy and soft, the universal indicators that he had woken me.

"Yes?"

"Good morning, my Sunshine, I hope you slept well."

"I WAS, until some inconsiderate person called and woke me… what do you want?" I tried to ignore the way my pet name rolled off his tongue, filled with so much admiration and love, but some more ice had melted from my frozen heart with each syllable.

"I'm sorry, love. I waited as long as I could stand it. I'm calling to ask, again, if you will have dinner with me tonight."

"Something tells me saying no would be a waste of my breath."

He chuckled lightly, responding, "Without a doubt."

"Fine, where?"

"Same place?" There was a pause, as I let that process in my foggy brain.

"You cannot be serious. After I ran out on my dinner? Um, NO."

"You choose, then. It's your town… pick your favorite."

"Like I can eat…"

"Well, let's hope. You need to eat." The concern in his voice was deafening, he knew that I had an eating disorder and had been painstakingly thin towards the end of high school. And God forbid that he was to discover that it was an issue that I continued to battle throughout my adult life. But for whatever weird reason, his concern rubbed me the wrong way. How dare he come here, after all this time, and act like he gave a damn about my daily caloric intake! The nerve of him to think he was entitled to be concerned for me at all!! My defenses flew back up, in full force, *Sunshine my ass*.

"Ya know what?? NO, I can't tonight, I forgot, I have plans."

Silence… after several seconds, he finally responded, his voice sounding wounded.

"Oh… well… okay. You got my hopes up for a second."

"I'm sure you will live through the disappointment."

"I'm so sorry that I'm responsible for this place that we find ourselves in. If we can just talk, really talk, I'm sure…" I cut him off.

"I'm just not ready to relive all this, and then to risk being hurt by you again, isn't even registering as a possibility I'm willing to consider. I'm sorry that you've wasted your time coming here."

"I've laid eyes on and had my arms around you... NOTHING is wasted in this trip. This is the most whole that I've felt in years."

Hearing him say that, made me acknowledge to myself that I felt the same way, but my fear of being hurt by him, again, was overwhelming any other thought I tried to have. His voice came again, when I hadn't replied.

"Why don't you take it easy, let things soak in for a bit. I understand that this was all very sudden for you, and I'm not going anywhere, I'll wait. Enjoy your plans for this evening." I could hear the teasing in his voice, revealing he knew, absolutely good and well, that I was lying and had no plans, but he was playing along with my excuse. He continued, "If you want to talk, call me. Other than that, I'll call you again in the morning."

"If you feel you must." I was being so hateful!

"I love you, Sunshine," he added, his voice sounding confident and resolved.

MELT

"K, bye."

As the snippy words left my mouth, my heart screamed, *I LOVE YOU, TOO!!! COME AND GET ME!! I NEED YOU, SO MUCH*!!! I tapped the end button before it could find its voice. No one needed to hear from my heart. Even I didn't talk or listen to it any more. I had bound it up tight and locked it away years ago. Guess some of the duct tape had come loose from over its mouth. I'd have to get that secure again, before any future contact with Jack occurred. If anything were allowed to slip out of my heart, my cover would be blown, and I'd be at his mercy. I had to find a way to regain firm control.

He was trying so hard to wear me down. He knew I could really dig in my heels and be stubborn, when my mind was set. I had made the act an art form. And my mind was set. At least I thought it was... I hoped it was. I could not allow myself to be hurt by this man again... I just didn't have it in me, there was no way I could survive it again. I was suspicious that my heart had been blabbing to my mind behind my back. And we couldn't have that. I got up, put my glasses on and headed into the bathroom.

If it was even possible, I actually looked worse than the night before. My hair was going in twenty different directions, lines were pressed into my face from the sheets, and there was a dried drool path from the corner of my mouth running down the side of my chin. Not to mention the impressive amount of crusties on my bloodshot eyes, so the eye boogers made it look as if I had a raging case of pink eye. "Sexy," I said, aloud, to myself. After going to the bathroom, I started the shower, and while waiting for the hot water to make its journey across the house, I went to the kitchen to make a cup of coffee. Naturally, the machine was low on water, so I filled it up to the top and waited for it to warm up, as I put the pod in and grabbed my favorite mug, a gift from my girls, with a lone "A" in elegant script on it. I placed it in the catcher's position on the machine. As I waited, his voice returned in my head, "I love you. I never stopped or wavered in that, EVER. Not one moment since high school, have I not loved you, please hear that. KNOW THAT." I shut the pod door and hit the button for the large cup. "**Get out of my head, Jackass**," I commanded, with loud authority, as I left the kitchen to get in the shower.

As I stepped into the shower the hot water felt comforting; like being in the company of someone you had known for years. All the tension left every muscle. Every worry and concern washed off and away, down the drain. My mind went blank, and I just stood in the haze of steam and vapor until the thought of his eyes, his beautiful deep-blue eyes, filled with pain and the tears in them, crossed into my memory. I turned, putting my face into the stream of the water jets to wash the vision from my mind. I stayed in till the water started to turn cold. First time in my life, I had read and followed the shampoo directions. I had rinsed and repeated, just to stay in longer. I had shaved my pits, legs, and bikini area, even though I had no plans to be in a swimsuit in the near future. I had scrubbed my heels with a pumice stone and thoroughly rinsed the soap out of my loofah... twice, as I had assured myself that I had seen a solitary trapped soap bubble. I had dried off completely, even making sure to reach every inch of my back. Then I carefully folded and hung my towel up.

I was stalling. My laptop was calling me... mocking me. I gave it a voice that I could hear clearly in my head, automated, English in dialect, and male. Just like the assistant on my phone. "You know you're curious about what more I have to share with you. I'm excited for us to spend the day together. Get comfy and come sit with me, love. I have so much for you to see... so much that you're dying to know. Answers, I have loads of them. Come cuddle with me." I shook the nagging thoughts from my brain, as I went to find clothes.

Sweats and a T-shirt were all that this day would require. For whatever reason, something possessed me... I pulled out the bottom drawer and reached deep to the bottom and all the way to the back and pulled out his old gym shirt. The very one I had not returned to my memory boxes, the night the girls and I had found it. I felt the need to hold it to my face and inhale deeply. It hadn't smelled like him for eons, but my recall could bring the proper fragrance back every time, from my long-term memory. I could not remember the name of the cologne, but the smell was forever burned in my mind. A wave of emotion came over me. I managed to block the tears, but not the goose bumps, as I slipped into my most cherished piece of clothing ever... His worn-out, stretched-out, cut-in-half, holey, old athletic T-shirt, that had always been too big on me. I remembered the day I had acquired it, like it happened yesterday.

I had been wearing his leather-sleeved, wool letterman's jacket. The sleeves hung three inches longer than my arms, and it smelled so heavily like him that I was pretty sure I spent most of my days intoxicated by a fog of pheromones. I had never told him, but I even slept in the damn thing many nights, just to feel close to him. Girls do some seriously silly crap in high school when they're in love. Can I get an "amen"?

I watched the end of football practice from the stands and had walked down to meet him at the field house afterwards. He emerged with this dirty, sweaty shirt tossed over his shoulder after changing back into his street clothes. It had fallen off as we were walking to his car, and I picked it up, since he was carrying all his things and mine, except my purse, as usual. After he put me in the car and was walking back around to get in, I had stuffed it inside the huge jacket to hide it. I had meant to return it (no, I didn't), whenever he asked if I knew where it was. But he had never mentioned it.

So, BOOM, here it was, all these years later, hanging from my shoulders and stopping just at the waistband of my sweats. It had been a crop top on him. Why guys had cut their shirts in half back then, I had no clue, other than to reveal their abs, which would be the most likely reason. And it achieved that purpose. They had all looked ideal after practice, a sexy kind of stinky physical perfection, that made the scenery on campus so much more enjoyable to soak in. Each a flawless, sweaty, newly created Greek god, in need of a name and an assignment to reign over, such as, Chloros, "god of grass stains." I was thankful the short sleeves had been left intact. Creating "muscle shirts" by removing them had also been all the rage. I took a brief glimpse of myself in the mirror, revealing a wet head and ratty attire, causing a small grin to cross my face, as I headed to fetch my almost certainly cold cup of coffee.

My coffee was indeed a bit cool, so I put it in the microwave for a few seconds, then unplugged my laptop, grabbing it off my desk, and headed for my favorite chair in the house—an oversized, overstuffed thinking spot with an ottoman. Its size had been perfect when the girls were little, for the three of us to pile up in to read their bedtime stories. Thinking I was most likely in for several hours of reading and crying, I returned to my room to grab the box of tissues off my bedside table. I considered making myself something to eat, maybe just a piece of peanut butter toast, but my nerves caused my stomach to flip upside down at the visual, so I passed. I plugged back into the wall then crawled into my chosen spot for the foreseeable future, with my laptop on my lap, as the computer's creators had always envisioned.

As I re-opened the newly revealed email account, my first order of business was to turn the chat "off." I would not be logged in to our old address, so I knew he would be watching here, probably as I was clicking, so I said out loud, "And watch me disappear." *CLICK*

I knew him well enough to know it wouldn't fly for long, he knew he was getting to me, breaking me down, so he would keep trying to sweet talk me until he had my full attention and had broken my will to fight. Turning chat off had put me on the clock. He would give me some time, but a new email would hit the inbox before I would need to get up to pee, I'd bet money on it. I got myself all comfy in my chair, my bare feet up on the ottoman and my freshly painted orchid toes dug under the throw that was lying across it. I made the long scroll back to the bottom of the list and clicked the next unopened email from where I had left off. I picked up my coffee from the end table, inhaled the aroma in a long, deep breath, as I began to read. It was dated only days after the previous entry:

My Sunshine,

My heart is hurting and so troubled still. I feel totally to blame, I should have never gotten so close to you! I'm so sorry. I think of you every moment of every day. I miss you more than I can express with words. And I want nothing more than for you to be healthy and happy! Sending my thoughts and prayers your way. I love you!

Well, okay, no tears on that one, maybe this was going to be easier than I thought. I took a minute and sipped on my coffee, looking out of the front window. Across the street, my neighbor was changing the oil of his prized antique muscle car in his garage. The sight brought a memory to my heart of another moment in Jack's and my long history, where I had blown the chance to be with him as more than friends, because of my stupid pride and insecurity. Like Sinatra, I have a few regrets.

It had been a nice day in early spring, our senior year. We had broken up a long time before, two years before to be exact, for absolutely no good reason. We had managed to become good friends several months after he had kicked the crap out of Brett… and after we had some emotional healing time, with neither of us willing to admit that we loved the other, or that we longed to be together again. This information had only come to light during our brief reconnection before his most recent exodus. I had pulled up at his house and he was working on his car, a white '78 Monte Carlo that was in really good shape. As I walked up the driveway, something, no, *someone* had caught my attention. It was Kimberly, a petite underclassman, with waist-long blonde hair. So much jealousy surged through my body, it was amazing that my skin had not turned visibly green. She was perched on a step, watching him work like a prissy, nosey, little bird. *OH, HELL NO*, I thought to myself. As I entered the garage, he greeted me.

"Hey, Sunshine, how's it going?"

Meekly, Kimberly added, "Hi."

I glared at her, then tilted my head and asked, "Don't you have anywhere else you could be?"

She looked away from my intimidating stare, towards him. "Um… yeah, I should probably go."

She returned her eyes to me, as I tilted my head to the other side, never taking my eyes off her, as I responded, "Probably," nodding my head in agreement, with a smirk that said, "get the hell out of here, and don't come back."

When she had walked out of earshot, he turned to me laughing quietly, and said, "That wasn't very nice."

I shrugged. "Today is my time with you, and I'm not sharing."

He cocked his head, raised his eyebrow and looked at me with intrigue, as if trying to read my mind. Oh, if he had only kissed me! Or even probed for more info! But he hadn't, and I ended the awkward gaze with, "What?" He just shook his head at me, then without another word, returned under the hood.

A few minutes later, he dropped the hood, loaded me into the passenger seat, and pulled out of the drive and out of the neighborhood. We spent the rest of the day driving, laughing, and eating. At one point, we stopped at a local park and played like little kids on the playground. He pushed me on the swings and caught me as I came down the slide. We rocked on the weird-looking animals that were mounted in the ground on huge springs. By the way, those will really get going when you're a big kid and have the weight to make them fully bend.

Then we took a short stroll around the small pond and fed the ducks our leftover fries. I was elated, when instead of heading home, he had stopped for snow cones. We had the best little mom-and-pop place in town that was only open while the weather was warm, and it had just opened the weekend before. He knew me so well, he had ordered for me without even asking me what I wanted. I remembered being completely at peace, content and happy the entire afternoon. A kiss never came, nor did either of us approach the subject of us returning to being more than friends. This missed opportunity was one of four that haunted me to this day. But the blame wasn't all mine, I came from a time when girls were supposed to play hard to get. I had thrown a pretty clear "come and get me" signal when I bounced Kimberly out, right? I mean, how thick can a guy be?

It was a rude awakening that my body was now flushed with jealousy and fury, as if the scene with Kimberly had just occurred this moment. My blood pressure soared, and my cheeks were red and hot. Also, I had the amazingly strong desire to jerk her blonde head bald! "Wow, that's just crazy!" I said, out loud. I found myself forced to acknowledge that my true feelings, no matter how deeply buried I had tried to keep them, were still very much alive, well, and fully possessive of him. All this time, and I was still head over heels, totally smitten with the boy. *DAMMIT.* Of course, this was only truly news to my deluded mind. Every ounce of the rest of my body responded with a deafening, *DUH*!!

I returned my focus to my laptop, clicking the next item up on the list, and an inspirational quote came up.

> **"The people who are meant to be in your life will always gravitate back towards you, no matter how far, or long they wander."**

Followed by a simple, "I love you." How true this seemed to be. Throughout our adult lives, we had continually seemed to come together out of nowhere, every so often. This pattern had started way before social media had made reconnecting with people so easily done. We had always managed to find each other, again and again, no matter how vast or dark the distance between us had been. Our hearts were drawn together like a magnet is to steel, always searching for, and pulling towards, the other. I had acknowledged this phenomenon so many times over the years, yet it still amazed me each time it happened.

The room was too quiet. I picked up the remote, turned the TV on, and went to the music channels. Great, now I was forced to decide what I was in the mood for. After scrolling through channels, I settled on soft classic rock. I was greeted by Bryan Adams singing "Everything I Do." The fact that this category now included the '80s made me cringe and feel old. I returned my attention to my laptop and clicked the mouse on the next item waiting to be opened. This one dated a week after the meme. Journey began to fill the air with "Open Arms," ironic. I almost smiled, almost. These arms were nowhere near beginning to open, much less, already being open. His, however, were open wide... as wide as they would stretch. I could visualize him standing, arms spread as wide as they would go, asking for a hug. The mental picture of my arms' position would look like I was wearing an invisible straight jacket. My arms were safe and securely wrapped around my torso, in a self-comforting hug. The open email was brief.

> **Things continue to be rough here. She is relentless and hateful. My memories are the bright spots of my days.**
>
> **Always**

That brought a huge lump to my throat. The thought of him being unhappy had always made me feel physically ill. The most painful part was knowing that they were both miserable, but neither one wanted to be the bad guy in their kids' eyes. I doubted that was the true issue for the Mrs., as "hateful" seemed to be her main mode of operation, she just needed the free pass to as much money as she could possibly get, from turning in her ring. And unfortunately, the check wasn't going to be big enough for her taste, unless she had something on him. She was willing to live in, and create, hell, until she got paid. It's possible they could've had a decent life together, but it had rarely been smooth, much less "happy." It seemed to be more of a restricted co-habitation than a marriage.

Moving right along… "click," next up, a month later, a real email:

> My Sunshine,
>
> I'm sorry it's been so long since I've been here. She's been following my every step, convinced that I am in contact with you. And she's still determined to prove that we were having an affair. I expected her to be this way, and that's the very reason why I will not try to reach you. She's spit enough venom on you, for no reason other than she had hoped you were her ticket to a divorce, and I will not risk placing you in the line of fire of her agenda. She finally was forced to accept and admit (to herself, NEVER to me) that she had discovered no more than a close friendship, and none of her "evidence" would stand in court as a violation. Pretty sure it was her

attorney that gave her the bad news. I only use the computers at the library to write to you: a server she has no access to. I know I'm probably being paranoid and going a tad bit overkill, but I must protect you, and do what is best for my kids, as well. So, I will continue to play my role and do what I'm told, all the while missing your laugh and encouragement. More than anything, I miss our friendship.

I focus on, and send my positive energy on to you, as I feel in my soul that you are still suffering. This thought is my daily torture. What a painful way to discover that you have a soulmate. How did we land here? We should be together with our own family. But then, perhaps, we wouldn't truly appreciate each other. Who knows? The regret is immense, but I try to focus on the future. Somehow, some way, I will hold you, unashamedly as my own, one day. This I pledge to us both. We will have our time, even if we're 80.

I'm here, always

"CHIME…" Stop the timer. There it was, just as I had predicted it would be, the new mail from his work email account (that I remembered seeing linked to his now nonexistent Facebook account). I took a deep breath, exhaling forcefully, slightly put out with the interruption and his apparent inability to keep his word to give me time and space. No sense in ignoring him, he would only start to flood me with more mail. I moved the cursor to the inbox link, so I wouldn't have to scroll all the way back up. When I opened it, I discovered that he was attempting to "chat" through email. It had been what, a whole two hours since our phone conversation?? Geez. Let me breathe, Jackass.

"How's my Sunshine?"

"Annoyed."

"Oh? How so?"

"Someone keeps bothering me with calls and messages. Trying to get me to go out with them."

"Give me a name, and I'll take care of him."

"Who said it's a him?"

A longer pause between new mail occurred, confirming that response had caught him off guard. HA!!

"Well played. Can we switch to chat, please? It's easier to have a convo…"

I turned chat on and typed:

"You said you were going to leave me be until tomorrow morning and it's been all of two hours."

"I missed you."

"After six years you should be used to that feeling."

PAUSE

"I could never get used to that feeling. Believe it or not, I actually did try to for a while, and it made me even more insane."

"Can I get back to what I was doing now, please?"

"Sure, but what do you think so far?"

"You need a hobby, if you've had all this free time."

"LOL! But am I scoring any brownie points?"

"Oh, I'm sorry, I wasn't aware that I was supposed to keep score.

But I guess it's in your favor, that I'm still willing to keep reading."

"Good! I'll take it! I really just wanted to remind you of something."

"And that is?"

"I love you."

"Yeah, so I've heard. TTYL."

"I'll take that as a promise. :)"

CRAP. I walked right into that.
CLICK Chat off.

As much as I hated to admit it, I missed him too, horribly. Seeing him again, the embrace, and of course, the kiss, had set free my girlie physical need for affection that I had buried with Brad. I found that I wanted to be close enough to feel his warmth, smell his scent, and hear his heartbeat. I wanted nothing more than to be held by him, deep in my core, I longed for it. *Shut up, stupid core.*

In the flux of communication that was there, I found pictures he had saved from my Facebook page of me and my girls, some of just me. Screenshots of posts I'd made, with comments he so desperately wanted to make on them but couldn't. Once I had dated someone long enough to change my relationship status to "in a relationship," and his response to the screenshot of the announcement was simply "HOLY HELL! JUST SHOOT ME NOW!" and it had made me laugh out loud. Then the following email had been filled with an apology, concern and well wishes, which brought the return of my tears.

> **Sorry I freaked out earlier. I want happiness for you. To see you truly content would make my world bearable, while breaking my own heart, at the same time.**

My relationship had only stayed semi-serious a couple of months. It's just hard to move on, when you don't actually have possession of your own heart, anymore. At some point, you wake up and have to acknowledge that you're wasting this good person's time, and your own. Not to mention, any lengthy involvement would lead to my girls being introduced and possibly becoming attached to this person. Not cool. I had to protect my girls' hearts more than my own. His comment to his screenshot of my status change back to "single" was only one word, "WHEW!!" Couldn't stop it, I laughed out loud, so hard. In the next letter, however, he had expressed his concern for me. Wondering if I had been hurt and sharing the gut-wrenching pain he felt with that possibility, followed by anger at the thought of "someone being stupid enough to dump you" had brought to him. And then, he had resigned himself to the more likely scenario that I had done the dumping; which led to the unloading of a landslide of emotional relief he felt, knowing I remained unspoken for.

It had been after that breakup that I decided not to date anymore. Too many people were desperate to find their happily ever after and I wasn't it for anyone, as I knew where my heart was eternally bound and chained. As I said earlier, I had sworn to myself there would be no more settling. I'd rather be alone than give someone only part of my heart again. I had stopped accepting any invitations to go out about this same time and just spent time with good friends. And those friends had finally stopped introducing other single friends to me in the hopes of making a match. I had actually made a sort of make-believe world to live in, within my own mind. I would simply pretend Jack was away on business and would someday return, but never actually buying into the fantasy that this day would ever come. Since the reality was that I was awake, and this was all happening, it made me want to pinch myself again. He was here, flesh and bone, living and breathing. The love of my life had returned from his last battle and had walked away from the war he had fought to survive, just so he could be with me at the end. Wow… So why was I having such a hard time trusting him, so we could get on with it? Why was I so terrified to finally get everything I had always wanted? I had to be "crazy or just plain stupid," as my grandma used to say.

But my fear of being hurt again was very real and more powerful than I had ever realized. It was almost paralyzing. It had taken on a life of its own and seemed so much larger and stronger than I had ever viewed myself. I had lived through losing him three times. I was 100% certain that I would not be able to survive a fourth. I had no clue what I could do to get him to understand that. I wondered if he could sense my fear as strongly as I was feeling his joy and hope. Did he have any idea how severely damaged I was? Any insurance company would mark me as a total loss. I would have to find a way to get him to see and understand this, so he would know his mission was doomed to fail. As soon as he did, he could move on and leave me to my memories and illusions.

The next item was a sweet memory of his, of a conversation we'd had, about the future.

> My Sunshine,
>
> I'm thinking today of a question that you asked me once. You sweetly asked why I had any desire to be with you, as you viewed yourself as less than worthy of my attention and devotion. I had no real answer at the time, and simply replied that "I just do." Do you remember? But now, after these years of being cut off from you, again, I have a real answer. That answer being: I'm incomplete without you. I'm lacking in everything good about being human. I'm low on laughter, happiness, love (obviously), hope, faith, intimacy, and above all... JOY. You are my JOY and THAT, my love,

is the reason I want... why I MUST
be with you.

Wishing that this finds you with all
the above abundantly present in
your world... well, I'm okay with
there not being intimacy, haha.

Forever Yours

My heart melted again. I did have all those things with
my girls, but like him, I had always felt like those emotions
were not present at the high levels that they could be. I
had plenty of room for more in each category. And now,
he had rekindled my longing for intimacy.

Great; that's exactly what I didn't need to fog up my
thinking at the moment.

Next, I was surprised to find a memory from high
school. You never think guys remember that far back, but
I guess that some do. They especially remember the things
that deeply impacted them. Girls tend to remember it all,
because everything deeply impacts us.

Do you ever think about the night
we went to see Chicago in concert?
It's amazing how often one of their
songs comes on, and it immediately
takes me back. I loved seeing you
so excited and happy! Having you
by my side and getting to hold your
hand or put my arm around you
when I wanted, I felt like the luckiest
guy in the coliseum.

Had I known that we wouldn't be
together much longer after that, I
would have done something to keep

the date going. Hell, I might have never taken you home! The way you kissed me goodnight had given me no indication that a breakup was on the horizon. I never understood what I had done wrong. I hope that someday you will tell me, as it's still a question that I ponder on, way too often.

Yours

He was right. I had never confessed to him the honest reason why I had broken up with him. The memory of that night rushed to my mind, again. My first concert and one of my all-time favorite bands, then, and to this very day; it had been an extremely thoughtful and loving gift, and the night had been perfect. I wouldn't have wanted to share the experience with anyone else. Unfortunately, it had been our last memory as a couple, as we had broken up just a week or so later, after my older brother, Josh, had drowned in a fishing accident.

I had never experienced heartbreak at that level. The surprising physical pain of the loss, not to mention the emotional, scared me so bad I had made an unhealthy and unrealistic decision to never allow myself to love anyone that deeply again, excluding those who were already at that depth in my heart. Jack had been the first victim in this new mindset. My feelings for him were already pressing against the point of no return, and I had to crush them before I was hurt. So, I had broken up with the excuse, with the lie, that I was interested in someone else. And I chose someone who was nowhere near attractive to me, so I wouldn't be tempted to get serious. It had worked, and by the time I had gotten over my childish reaction to losing Josh, Jack no longer showed any interest outside of friendship, so I assumed that he had no true, lasting feelings for me, and I had made do with us just being friends. It was better than the alternative of not having him in my life at all. Hindsight is always 20/20, I had been a moron.

The next entry was another screenshot of one of my Facebook posts. I had been sick, VERY sick, and was asking my friends to pray for me, as I didn't want to land in the hospital, away from my girls. As it turned out, I had pneumonia, and only by my pleading with my doctor, and my awesome mother-in-law swearing that she would be with me twenty-four seven, did he agree to let me stay home. It had all started with my asthma, that I was always stubborn about and chose to ignore whenever possible. It had developed into bronchitis (that I still tried my best to ignore), then, bam! I had pneumonia. Seriously, start to finish I was sick and coughing like a chain smoker, for the best of eight weeks from first wheeze to last. Albuterol had become my constant companion, and my mother-in-law swore that my entire oxygen-deprived body sported an icky blue hue for a month. Jack had commented after the screenshot…

I am so worried about you, I'm beside myself. It's not in your nature to direct attention to yourself, or ask anyone for anything, so I know that you must be scared! I would give anything to be there with you to take care of you. My heart is aching and I feel so helpless. I am praying for you and wishing you the speediest of recoveries!! And I'm also praying that you drop your stubbornness, and do as you are told, until you are well!! Yeah, I KNOW you and your SASS!! Try to behave…

He had continued to make an entry every day following, until he had grandly announced his relief in seeing that I was healthy again. And how very much he wished he could take me out to celebrate.

Several quick "touching base" and "thinking of you" entries followed. Then I opened another memory from our dating days, one I was floored that he remembered. It happened to be one of my most favorite memories of "us," and one that I thought back on often, as I found comfort and peace in it. Living on a farm, with livestock, my family had acres and acres of pasture land. One cold evening in February, Jack and I had driven out on a three-wheeler as far from the house and lights as we could be and still be on my family's property. We had brought a boom box and thrown out a blanket and then covered ourselves with another one, neither had been very heavy. The boom box had my favorite mix tape in the cassette player. I had recorded many of my favorite artists and bands including .38 Special, Journey, Bon Jovi, Chicago, Luther Vandross, and of course, our song by Kenny Rogers was among the mix. We had lain and talked for hours, looking at the stars, and intermittently making out, of course, until the sound of my daddy's .357, being fired twice, alerted us that we were well past my curfew. Ahhhh, the days before cell phones. I had often wondered if he remembered it as well as I did, or at all. What I read answered my question with a resounding YES, HE DID.

Last night I dreamt about that night we went out in the pasture at your parents' house to stargaze. It felt so real, that when I woke I was confused by my surroundings and heartbroken not to find you beside me. I recalled how nervous I had been to touch you. We had kissed several times before that night, but we had never truly made out. My mind still remembers the texture of your bra, which seems crazy, after all these years. How we didn't freeze to death under that thin blanket, once both of our shirts were off, is a mystery. The music was even there, playing in the background, "You're the Inspiration," to be exact, then it had been followed by our song. My heart raced in my dream, just as it had that night when you began unbuttoning my shirt, and then it exploded as it went on to the moment you had allowed me to unbutton yours. I swear I could feel your skin against mine and the lace trim of your bra brushing up against my chest. I heard your voice clearly when you reprimanded me with, "NO, SIR," when I made a move to unclasp it. Your control was always stronger than mine. I remembered how you surprised me when you had unbuttoned my jeans. At the time, I don't think that you realized that your fingertips had brushed against "me," and I had to recite the Pledge of Allegiance in my head, to keep from making a mess in my boxers. Stop laughing, I'm serious. Lying on top of you with every line of our bodies pressed together, was rougher on me than any teenage boy should have to endure and having your arms (and legs at some points) wrapped around me, pulling me closer, had been torture in its simplest form. But torture I was more than willing to endure. I welcomed it, even. I wanted you so badly, it was all I could do not to scream. I was so euphoric I felt drunk, right up until your dad starting shooting. At that moment, I had become sober immediately; which by the way, is the point at which I woke up.

After I regained my bearings and was firmly awake, and back in my horrible reality, I lay there and remembered how beautiful and clear the sky had been that night. How I had pointed out constellations, and you had asked me to pick out a star, for it to be "ours." A feeling of peace washed over me with the memory of your head resting on my shoulder and having my arms wrapped around you. I can't tell you how many times I've recalled that night. Each and every time that I've noticed that the sky was perfection a chilly night, my mind wanders back there.

Every. Single. Time.

I contemplated on if I should tell him that I had, in fact, been aware that night that I had touched him. That I had done it on purpose, even, trying to drive him insane; which apparently had worked. I had little doubt that if my daddy hadn't interrupted us, my virginity would have been surrendered right there, on our farm, that night. I had wanted him as bad, or possibly even more, than he wanted me. I had always wished that it had been him that I had taken that first major intimate step with. The memory made me smile, and warmth washed over me. I decided to keep my secret to myself, to let him keep thinking my teasing touch had been unintentional.

I spent the next few hours reading, with only pee breaks and one failed attempt at eating. I could never eat when I was stressed, or I would simply forget to try. I had been that way for as long as I could remember; a forever lingering symptom of my lifelong battle with my eating disorder. I read each and every thought he had felt like sharing with me over the last six-plus years, as they were lovingly logged there. Some were deep professions of devotion, others just basic "how I wish I could share this awesome day with you," along with far too many "this day totally sucked ass, and I wish you were here to make it better." All the years I had worried and wondered about him, he had documented for me, his life, as well as mine. I viewed it all as a precious and very thoughtful gift; one that I would keep forever, even if we went our separate ways. His thoughts would forever be my most prized possession. No one had ever given me anything more precious.

II

TABLE FOR ONE

Early in the evening, before dark, there was a knock at the door. Who in the world could that be? I peeked through the peep hole, and SWEET CRAP!! There he was... my new stalker. He was relentless! Handsome and perfect, but relentless! UGH! I came down off my tiptoes, shaking my head in disbelief. I ran my fingers through my hair to fluff as much as possible, as I had just let it air dry that morning. I pinched my cheeks to hopefully bring some color to them, and licked my lips for that soft, wet look. *That's as good as this is going to get,* I thought. Then an evil and ornery idea came to mind.

"Who is it?"

"It's me, Sunshine..."

"JACK??"

"Ummmm... No..."

Gotcha. I couldn't stop myself from grinning as I opened the door, but I quickly regained my straight face, before he saw me. There he stood. The setting sun behind him made him glow like an angel, pure perfection. Even with his age showing, my heart still saw him as eighteen, flawless and beautiful. His voice slapped me out of my swoon.

"YOU stole my shirt!" His eyes were wide with recollection and recognition, as a half grin appeared across his face.

"And YOU have a serious issue with understanding the premise of leaving someone alone." His laugh was musical, still my favorite sound in the whole world to hear.

"Yeah... Sorry about that. I'll try to do better. It's just that I was worried that, if history serves my memory correctly, you wouldn't eat because you're stressed. So..." He held up a pizza box with a bouquet of daisies resting across the top. Then from behind his back, he produced a bottle of my favorite wine. Wow, he had remembered my preferences all this time.

SWOON

What a jackass. I kept myself from reaching for them and just tilted my head in a silent question.

"Oh, I don't want to stay... well, I mean I DO WANT to stay, but I understand... I just came by to give you these, and now I'll go." With that added clarification of his intention, I accepted my gifts, and he turned to go. Suddenly he spun back around, kissed my forehead and said, "You look sexy as hell, by the way, even if you are a thief." He gave me that crooked little grin and my heart skipped at least three beats. He turned again to leave, and hollered back, "Tell this Jack dude that he has some serious competition!" He got in his truck and pulled out. I stood there dazed and frozen like an idiot, unable to move until his taillights disappeared down the street. I closed the door and walked to the kitchen.

His taillights had brought back a harsh memory. I was back in my apartment all those years ago, on that night, the only time we had ever slept together. After finally arriving together in a perfect moment in time, we had made long overdue love. A brief moment of peace and all being right in the world. The same night I had remembered last night at dinner, THE night, as I always referred to it. To this memory I could remember every word, touch, kiss (and their placement), every heartbeat, every breath. It was the most complete I had ever felt. Yet it had ended abruptly, with tears and taillights reflected in the window, as he had driven away with the feeling of obligation to marry the woman who didn't have his heart. And I had then returned to, and fell for, the man who would later become my best friend, husband, and the father of my children. The first man I had ever loved was gone. He was married and never coming back. I had resigned myself to that, and I had moved on. Those taillights were burned in my mind forever, as a reminder that I wasn't wanted by him, that I wasn't the one he had chosen.

I found a vase and put the flowers in water, and they now loomed in front of me, teasing me, like they knew I was caving. I grabbed a glass and opened the wine. I poured a glass, then took a huge swig straight out of the bottle. As I opened the pizza box, my mind responded with *that jackass,* when I saw the pepperoni with onion, mushrooms, and extra cheese, again, my favorite. I picked the best-looking slice, you know, the one with the most cheese, the biggest mushrooms, and the pepperoni with the slightly toasted edges. There is always one perfect slice in every pizza.

My husband had loved this pizza, too. At least, I assumed he had, he told me he did; maybe he only acted like he loved it because it made me happy and he loved me. This thought caused me to think back and recap my adult life. In hindsight, I could see now that Brad had always gone to great lengths where my happiness was concerned. And for a time, I managed to have a good life. I had been happy. He was a good man, totally in love with me.

As I reflected, I still felt guilty, but was thankful he never had any clue of the secret I kept hidden in my heart. I had done a really good job of keeping it buried deep.

After all, my feelings carried no weight in my real life. I reminded myself that at the time, there was no reason for me to doubt that Jack had been able to salvage his marriage and was now happy, thus, why he was still married; never giving me a second thought. He was with the girl that he chose to spend his life with, and that girl was not me. With little difficulty, I accepted that as being fact, when he abandoned me after I had surrendered my body, in a selfless offering, to him (the love of my life). At the same time, I had broken my strong moral code. Brad and I had not formally "committed" to each other at that point, but it still wasn't something I would ever consider doing, committed or not. But it had been HIM, the single person in this world who could change the tide in my little world, with just a smile.

As time passed, I'd grown to feel used and convinced myself that I was no more than a piece of ass to him; one last wild oat to sow before going to the altar. I had never been able to listen to "My Heart Can't Tell You No" since. It had been pure torture for months, when Sara Evans had re-released it. I avoided country stations like the plague, until it faded from popularity.

We hadn't even spoken of this night, a couple of years later when he took me to dinner, before I got married. With all my new information, I could now guess that the memory was also painful for him, as he had never seen me cry over him, before then.

After that dinner, I had managed to master my "ignore it and it will go away" mind-set, and it served me well up until my girls had been born, and I had my hands full. With full-time distractions, I didn't have time to think about my heart anymore; being solely concerned about theirs. The years passed fairly quickly afterwards, with birthdays and holidays coming and going. I was very content. We had laughter and love in our home, and I couldn't ask for more than that. The girls brought me so much joy, and I felt safe and loved, however still incomplete. Keeping so busy, I was able to ignore the nagging from my soul and go on with each day like all was perfect in my little world, and in a way, it was. We were the typical American family. We stayed busy with dance recitals, homework, and enjoyed our time away together to the beach, camping, cruises, and numerous week-long vacations. We were blessed.

The worst day of my life, the day Brad was late getting home, and a state trooper arrived on our porch that evening, hat and tie on, had happened during year ten. Our whole world was upside down, in a matter of a few simple words spoken by this stranger in uniform. Brad was gone, and I was a widow with young children, daddy's girls... I was alone. My biggest goal, and focus, became getting my girls through it as emotionally intact as possible. The funeral, and the months following, were all a blur. I had been desperately exhausted but determined to be strong enough to get them safely through the mental trauma caused by losing a parent, so very young. They slept with me for months... then when I thought they had returned to their own beds, I discovered they were still sleeping together; one going to the other's bed at some point, after they thought I was asleep, in a planned, joint effort to appear strong, for me. My precious girls had put on a brave face for me and had tried to carry me, as I had carried them through this adjustment. I had been so focused on them, I didn't notice that I was obviously struggling and not fooling anyone. But time stops for no one, and eventually, thankfully, we had found our way.

I remembered that it had been a little over a year after Brad was killed, when a few friends encouraged me to step out into the waters of social media. It didn't take long for me to reconnect with Jack and begin talking, and for the first time in forever, I had felt whole again. It started out slow, just catching up on where our worlds were at the time. Then over several months, the chats became more frequent, until daily was the norm, and completely platonic. He had become my closest friend, my confidant, sounding board, voice of reason and cheerleader; you name it, that's what he was to my world. Then his wife discovered our closeness and spun her head around. She had called and berated me, and when I stopped answering the calls, she had left venom-filled messages, demanding that I send her copies of anything I had from him or she would destroy my family, by informing my husband of her discovery; which in reality, was nothing but a close friendship. I remembered thinking *go ahead, call the dead man, tell him I said hello*! I had apologized for any overstepped boundary, even though I knew we had not crossed any line; respecting their union. Did I love him? Sure. Did he still love me? Possibly, I guessed. But he was married. We were just friends, end of story.

We had never had contact since. I felt so sorry for him. How awful it must be, to have someone follow your every move! And then I was shocked and a little disappointed in myself, to discover that I felt pity for her as well. How insecure and miserable of a person must you be, to feel you have to go digging and spying all the time, what a sad life! It was pathetic, actually, and a pitiful excuse for a relationship. Then anger had quickly replaced any sympathy as her words sank in, "send me everything." She didn't want me away from her husband, she wanted ammunition to use against him, most likely, to use as cause to divorce him. Those words had been what convinced me that she wanted out too, but she also refused to make the initial step to end it and risk being hated by their kids, or some less understandable twisted reason. I never understood why divorce had to be so ugly. Why people would stay together instead of being adults saying, "Hey, sorry this didn't go as we planned, I wish you well," and then move on in a healthy way for their children. This home situation had to be one covered in eggshells, and that broke my heart.

His happiness was all that mattered to me, far outweighing my own. From that moment on, she had become the one single person that I loathed on this entire planet. I never could wish bad things towards her though. I would never want his children to go through pain like my girls had lived through, losing their dad. But I could openly admit to myself, that if she was in a crosswalk in front of me, it would end poorly for us both. Thank God for distance.

One point was very clear to me. She had no comprehension of the depth of love that I held for him, or she would have known that there was no way in hell that I would ever help her damage a single hair on his head, much less have a hand in destroying his life. Any human that loves another should feel that way. And she obviously did not feel this way about him, as she wanted to destroy him. Not once did she demand that I leave her man alone and go away; which spoke volumes. You don't prepare to walk out over little to no information, entirely innocent information, mind you, when you love the person you're with. You dig in and fight for what you want to keep, period. She was willing to walk way too easily if she was given all she felt entitled to... sad. To spend such a significant piece of your life truly unhappy, what a waste! And I knew for certain, these feelings were decades old. To my recollection and understanding, trouble had started early in the marriage, and real happiness had occurred few and far between, during its history.

My marriage may not have been my ultimate dream, but at least I could honestly say that we were happy and content together. I was devastated when Brad died. He had been my best friend, someone who thrived on bringing me joy and who seemed to gain joy from doing so. He was someone that I looked forward to spending time with, and I had no problem with the thought of growing old with him. He had been an amazing husband and father. Another reason I had not rushed out to find a serious relationship: that father act would be hard for any man to follow, and my girls deserved the quality they were used to. With them recently turning 16, I only hoped that they remembered enough about how their dad had treated us all, and that they would expect and demand the same from any suitor.

Their junior year was just around the corner; not very much time was left at home with me. Then, what? I would be totally alone, for the first time in decades. I always poured all my energy and focus into my girls, that way, I didn't have to think about my situation. And now, my perfect, constant distractions were about to leave the nest; they already had busy lives of their own that took them away on a regular basis. I would need a new plan and very soon. What a coincidence that Jack would surface. Thinking of the girls' ages made me realize that his youngest would have graduated last year. He was all done, technically speaking. No visitation schedule, or communication with the ex-wife, he was free from her, outside of the major life events of his kids; things like weddings and grandbabies being born, and then their birthday parties. That must be quite a feeling after all these years.

I was so deep in thought that I jumped when my phone rang. It was one of my closest friends from home, Margo. We had hardly spoken in high school, but in recent years I had become tight with a group of female classmates; all whom I would now die for. We even began calling ourselves the HighLites, as most of our group chose to color our now-graying hair. Margo was one of the charter members.

I said "hello," and she responded with, "Are you alone?" I'd completely forgotten that I had shared my dinner plans for the night before, with her and one other from the group, Faith; who also happened to be my sister-in-law, as she was married to Will. I'd grown a bit closer to these two in recent time, not by choice, it just kind of played out that way. Over the years, we had each stepped up in our roles to each other, depending on the need and what we all had going on. It just happened that they got deeper in this part of my business than the others. The rest of our entourage would be filled in the next time we were all together, which usually worked out to be a couple of times a year, at the least. If I didn't end up coming clean before that opportunity.

"Of course, I'm alone… you think I'm easy?"

"Well…" I had to laugh, I adored Margo's humor.

"Hang on a minute," she said, "let me add Faith on three-way."

"Three-way??? You **DO** think I'm easy."

"Well… Hang on."

That was a good idea, at least I wouldn't have to repeat the events of the last twenty-four hours, more than the one time. However, the three of us trying to talk over each other on a conference call was going to be comical.

Margo's voice returned. "Okay, are we all here?" Faith and I replied, then I greeted my sweet friends.

"It's so sweet of y'all to call. How are things?? Having a nice weekend?"

"Yeah, yeah," came Margo again. "Cut the crap, enough with the stalling, you know why we're calling, SPILL."

Faith added, "Yeah, girl, don't keep us waiting on pins and needles, we want

DETAILS! First of all, how long were you together?"

"About thirty minutes."

Margo responded with, "Damn! I lost! I owe you ten, Faith!"

A brief spot of laughter followed, after I reprimanded them for having placed bets on my love life, then I began to relay the play-by-play. My girlfriends were very supportive. Never interrupting, only adding in sighs and an occasional comment like, "I was afraid that would happen," and "bless your heart." However, Margo did lighten the mood as I relayed how he initially kissed me, when she inquired if tongue had been involved. Faith had just giggled at the question, but in a way that I could tell she wanted the answer too, which, by the way, was NO. It always felt good to talk about him with people who knew him. I felt like he was not as real to my two close friends here that I had shared him with. I was always concerned that they thought I was making him up, like I had an imaginary boyfriend that I was entirely infatuated with. However, that would be the perfect excuse not to date. The idea had crossed my mind more than once, and I could pull off the charade until people wanted to meet him. I could never discover a way around that problem. You can only put people off for so long, before they get wise to the truth.

When I finished telling my tale, Faith was first to respond with, "Are you okay? I hate that you're by yourself, I wish we could be there with you."

"Oh, I'm not alone. Apparently, he has an inability to leave me alone and cannot stay away. Believe me, I've tried." I laughed, lightly.

Then Margo asked, "So, what's the plan?"

"I was hoping you were calling to tell me, any ideas?"

"Well, I'm praying for ya." God had her parents name her "Faith" for a reason. She was our official spiritual leader. She went on, "I know that you're scared to death of being hurt again, but I also know that you love him more than most people ever love anyone who's not their blood."

"That's true," entered Margo. "So, the question isn't: do you still love him, we all know the answer to that one. The real one is: do you trust him enough to let him love you?"

I realized, in that moment, that Luther Vandross was singing "Don't Want to be a Fool" in the background. Seriously, it was like my life had a soundtrack.

"I just don't know what I'm gonna do. Him being here and saying all that he's saying, is like a dream come true.

After wishing for this to happen for so long, now that it is, I'm having a hard time accepting it as reality. I'm so angry with him. But I know firsthand what life is like for me without him, and I really don't want to return to that type of existence. However, I'm so damaged now… so hurt. I just don't know if we have enough time left on this planet for him to repair that, ya know?"

Margo was the first to respond. "Just the fact that he's THERE, in person, speaks volumes about what he's willing to risk, to get that chance. It took some balls to show up before even making a feeler call."

"Yeah, it did!!" responded Faith, "BIG ones! What if you had told him to step off?

All that time and money wasted! He must be crazy!" I just laughed lightly… he DID have to be crazy.

Then Margo chimed in with exactly what I was thinking… "He IS crazy… about YOU. There's no mystery about that anymore."

"Truth," Faith responded.

Tears came to my eyes as I said, "I do wish y'all were here… or I was there. I could use a hug."

"Bless your heart," and "Poor thing," came simultaneously.

Then Faith, again, with, "Girl, you cry if you need to cry, we're here for ya."

So, I did. Nothing was said for the couple of minutes that I let it out… but I heard sniffles, so I knew my friends were crying with me. They knew my heart and knew that I was in a tremendous struggle, almost more than I could bear. Before we hung up, I reminded Faith that I wasn't ready for my brother to know what was going on, and asked again, that she keep Jack's presence, here, to herself. She hated keeping stuff from Will, they had NO secrets, but with my promise that I would tell him soon, myself, she agreed. We told each other "I love you" and said our goodbyes, after I promised I would at least text with updates.

135

Then Margo threw in, "Don't sleep with him until he's earned it, no matter how bad ya want to!! BYE!!"

"Oh my goodness!! BYE!!"

I could hear them both laughing as I tapped the red receiver icon on my phone screen. I shook my head as I thought about those two, completely off their leashes and out of bounds, but spot on in their summations. I wondered how the other three girls, Courtney, Sarah, and Savannah would feel when they were brought up to speed. They were also well aware of my feelings for Jack and all that transpired over the years between us. But they had encouraged me during my depression to let it go and move on... I knew that my inability to do so caused them concern and frustration, so I tried my best to avoid speaking of my continued struggle and tried to be "normal" around them; I hated to disappoint them. My guess was they would not be surprised. We all knew each other very well, and any attempt to hide or cover any emotion was usually moot, as the others would always see through it. Because of this well-known fact about our group bond, I was not surprised that Margo and Faith had totally seen through my facade and called it exactly as it was.

My heart totally belonged to this man now. There was no denying that. He had held a large piece of it since the first time he spoke to me, in what seemed like another lifetime ago, so denial was impossible; especially now that all restrictions were removed, and I had total confirmation that his feelings for me were equal to mine for him. Having to acknowledge that I had never been a great liar, trying to deny it would be wasted time and breath. Setting my phone down, I picked up my second piece of pizza and slowly took a bite. I hardly noticed the taste, as I continued to think of the dilemma I was in. The truth is, that just because you love someone, and they love you, it doesn't necessarily mean that you can, and should, be together. Sure, if things go well, it can be the best thing ever. But we had already been through so much bad… so much pain and loss, could a real, adult, relationship between us even work? And how awful it would be, if we were to jump in and discover the answer was "no." I could not even fathom that idea. It would destroy me.

As things were, I was unfulfilled and lonely, but I still had my fantasy of my prince being out there. Knowing that my knight in shining armor could come swooping in to rescue me and make it all better at any minute, had become where my sanity rested. I felt blessed in that I had an actual real face on my prince, so many girls don't. Just some random handsome face attached to the dictionary definition of the perfect body, a mirage. The irony was that it was happening! My prince was here, with his sword drawn, asking for my hand so he could pull me up onto his perfect white steed and ride off into the sunset with me! And yet, I'm standing there with my hands in my pockets, looking at him like he's nuts. Dude even showed up with flowers, pizza, and wine, now that's romantic. But I was unmoved. I honestly didn't have any idea what my gut was telling me. My fear was drowning out all possible use of reason. I felt no sense of direction. You would think after wanting something so badly for so long, the answer would be easy. Why was I struggling with this? Again, I questioned if I was the one who was crazy. I had to be a few short steps to certifiably insane.

I didn't quite finish the second slice. I realized he had only brought me a small, as he knew that if I ate at all, that it wouldn't be much. How could I even *consider* turning away someone who knew me so well? I started to refill my wine glass but stopped after the first splash hit the bottom. I said, "Screw it," out loud, shot back the splash, then took the bottle with me back to my comfy chair. "Now, where was I?" I said again, out loud, to myself. I clicked the next item on the screen.

Sunshine,

I feel the need to tell you how incredibly proud I am of you for going back to college!! THAT'S MY GIRL!! I had no idea that you have a love for English, but if that's what tickles your fancy, then I support you! Not an easy major, I would assume, with an insane amount of writing, I'm told. I wish you so much luck, and I know that you will do very well! You always under estimated yourself when we were in high school. You're so incredibly smart! Can't wait to follow this process, and I wish I could be with you as you undertake this new journey!

I returned to college, attempting to boost my self-esteem and confidence. Dropping out after high school, I had always told myself that I failed because it was too hard for me. Even after rocking technical school, I managed to brainwash myself into believing that, somehow, it had been easier work. The reality was that I had never devoted any time to studying in college. I would rarely go to class, then show up for tests that I had not prepared for, and be amazed when I would fail them, or best case, I would score a D. I never studied in my entire academic life. I skated through high school with C's, which required little-to-no effort on my part. I had easily accepted myself as being of average intelligence. The truth is that no one is born knowing everything, and that one learns from listening and reading, a LOT. I realized now, that I made it through high school simply on what I soaked in during class, only half paying attention and I had tried to proactively instill good study habits in my girls, which seemed to be working quite well, to this point. I finished my degree and brought up my failing GPA to just barely over a 3.0 before graduation; carrying a 3.8 at the institution. When I later shared my low self-esteem concern with my friends, they told me that I was completely stupid to ever think that I was stupid. Wait... whaaa??

I closed the entry, feeling pretty good about myself and took another large swig of wine.

> Sunshine,
>
> It's Friday night and I'm off to watch my nephew play in his final high school football game. It's brought back memories of our games.

I was distracted from reading by the song changing on the TV: "Heaven" by Bryan Adams. I was seriously starting to wonder if God was playing DJ just to mess with me and have a good giggle. I shook my head and returned my attention to the laptop screen.

> I used to love to look back at you up in the stands, and I was always thrilled if I caught you looking at me, too. Which you usually were. I was always worried about you being cold in those short skirts, but at the same time, loved how the cold made your cheeks rosy. You looked beautiful. I was pissed every time that dude you were dating was there. He never seemed to offer you

his jacket (to cover your legs with) during your break. He was such an ass-wipe! I hated that guy!

Then, there was the game that you passed out in the stands, UGH! It had been all I could do to make myself stay on the side-lines. I was punished with running like... 50 "hills" for turning my back on the game, even though we were killing the other team and there were only a few mins left. I wish we had still been dating, all of those games. There is so much I would go back and do differently, if I could. But I guess it's crazy to even think about. We can never go back, and we are where we are and can only hope to make things right in the future. I'm praying I get that opportunity in this life.

Always

I remembered all the games as well. Once the girls had started high school and were on the dance team, the memories had been frequent and inescapable. There was always a kid wearing his number, and I would cheer for that boy as loud as if I were his momma. And his memory served him well, as I had always been looking at him. It was my only opportunity to do so, without being obvious to everyone else. When he was on the field, I would hold my breath every play. One awful night, he had been hurt. It took every ounce of control for me not to cry while the paramedics worked on him. The relief I felt, when he raised his thumb to the crowd while being rolled off the field on a gurney, flushed through my body again like it had just happened in this moment. He had messed his knee up, bad, and was out for the season. He spent the remaining games on the sidelines, on crutches. He looked so sweet and helpless to me. I had to physically fight the urge to hug him, every time I saw him during the school day, as I wished I was able to take care of him.

The wine had started to kick in, and I was beginning to have trouble focusing. I caught myself remembering the one year we had a "powderpuff" flag football game, where the cheerleaders and drill team played against the same groups from a rival high school. The football team had been our coaches, so Jack and I had spent some bonus time together. I looked forward to practices, knowing I would get to see him, and if instruction required it, he would have to touch me to teach me, by positioning my body into the correct posture and stances required for me to play well and not hurt myself. Several times I used the excuse that I was cold, to explain the goose bumps that would cover my arms any time he touched me. Even if he placed his hands on my shoulders during a pep talk, I'd flush head to toe, and the bumps would be visible immediately. The guys had done an exceptional job, and we defeated the other team handily. Everyone had gone out to celebrate the victory at the pizza place, but knowing that I would just be miserable that close to him without being "with" him… I made an excuse and went straight home.

This was about the time I started struggling with my eating and received a full-blown eating disorder diagnosis during the year that followed. I'd grown so thin by the next fall that I appeared tiny and fragile. I wore baggy sweaters to hide it but was discovered when my momma had entered my bedroom, with a walking-in knock, to discover me in my bra, changing uniforms before the game that night. She gasped in shock and horror, at the sight of my ribs being highly visible in my back and screamed for my daddy. Back then, we didn't talk about disorders like we do now… they were considered private matters. My momma threatened to put me in a facility for treatment and "embarrass me thoroughly," while my daddy promised a beating like I had never seen, if I didn't get control of it and "cut that shit out." The fear of my parents had been enough to make me get myself under sufficient control and I was able to gain some weight to pacify them.

Jack voiced his concerns several times at how thin I was and was concerned that I was sick. I had always been able to convince him that I was just really busy and rarely hungry. He caught on at some point and began arriving to our lunch group with food for me. Chicken nuggets with nacho cheese sauce for dipping. Sounds disgusting, but it was really good, and he knew that I liked it. He would then be relentless throughout lunch until I had eaten a good portion, by throwing food at me, insisting that I attempt to catch it in my mouth, his playful way of force-feeding me. It was only in recent years of therapy that we discovered that this disorder, most likely, took root in Josh's death. I'd buried the pain, pretending to be okay for the sake of my parents, they needed me to be strong. I shared this revelation with my mom after therapy, and she explained that she had considered Will and I needed counseling afterward, but we both seemed to handle it very well, so she had stopped fretting over it. Just a word to the wise: If you know a child who loses someone close to them, no matter how good they may appear to recover on their own… they are NOT okay!

A few entries further down, he shared one of his memories. One that I did not have stored as well, and my heart broke as I read through the pain he carried from this single evening from our youth—prom. We had been only friends for the previous two years, so naturally, we had other dates for the big event. Honestly, I had to admit that I had no recollection of who his date had been, or even a mental picture of seeing him, that night. My only guess as to why I had no recall, would be that I was so jealous that I blocked the memory from long-term storage. His words revealed that he suffered from the complete opposite problem with his recollection of the event. He remembered every detail.

A song came on today and it took me back to our prom. I've never shared with you how awful of a memory that night is for me. Even after trying to mentally prepare myself for the evening, for weeks ahead of time, seeing you there hit me like a ton of bricks. You had been dating the guy that escorted you for a long time. So long, in fact, that I had given up hope of ever getting you back. I tried to make peace with the idea that we would only be friends for the rest of our lives.

I'd done pretty well in the early parts of the evening. Picking up my date and suffering through what seemed like forever of taking pictures. Then, throughout dinner, I managed to talk and laugh with the rest of the group of our classmates that she and I met up with at the restaurant. But deep down, I was relieved that you had apparently chosen to eat elsewhere. We arrived at the hotel and I was thankful that there was still no sign of you. We had our obligatory professional picture taken and moved on inside the ballroom. Some of the same group from dinner, mostly my closest friends, all settled at one table and had continued with the banter and laughter from dinner. I remembered wishing my date wouldn't sit so close. I actually began to worry that something had happened to you, when it started to get well past the starting time and you still had not entered the room.

Then, suddenly, there you were. Beautiful is not a strong enough word for how you looked. I had been mortified when you decided to cut your long, long hair up to your ears, but I had to admit that the look worked on you as well as the long hair had. That asshole that you were dating was smiling like the cat that swallowed the canary, with you on his arm. I immediately wanted to punch him in the mouth. You were smiling too, more in an uncomfortable way, but that quickly changed as our friends came up to greet you, and real joy soon appeared in your expression. Your shoulders were bare, revealing the skin (I knew to be overly soft) that was glowing, with just a hint of tan. It was complemented perfectly by the pale pink color of your dress. You looked as if you had just stepped out of one of my many daydreams. Then, as you began talking with your hands, the way you always do, I noticed the one piece of jewelry, other than a pair of small earrings, that you chose to wear... the charm bracelet I gave you. My heart swelled and broke at the same time. I questioned in my mind why you would choose to wear it here? Was there a deeper meaning behind it than the simple possibility that you liked the way it looked with your dress? Should I take it as a sign that I meant more to you than just a friend?

I became so distracted by my thoughts that my table mates started doggin' on me. My date even reached under the table and squeezed my knee, to bring my attention back to the table. I had somewhat rudely taken her hand and returned it to her own lap and then scooted my chair over a few inches away from her, declaring it to be "hot in here." As you walked deeper into the room, I couldn't help but follow your every move. As much as I knew you didn't care for being a girly girl, you were so elegant and graceful in your movements. The heels you were wearing were a great accessory to your incredible legs. I always loved your legs. Your sweet knees above your athletic calf muscles, leading down to your dainty ankles and small feet, were always a distraction when you were in uniform over the years. Some girls don't have ankles and look like Miss Piggy in heels. Not you, your legs rocked like a runway model's. I had a hard time keeping my eyes off of you the entire night, except during the slow dances. Having to witness that dude putting his arms around you, ballad after ballad, was unbearable. Then once he kissed you, and the rage and jealousy had climbed to a level that I'm surprised, to this day, I had managed to contain. I lost count of the times I killed that asshole in my head, before you two left. My date tried to get me to leave several times before, but there was no way I was leaving, with you still there. I had such little time left to have you in my sight, and I swore to myself that I wouldn't miss a moment of it.

Graduation was quickly approaching, and the thought of not seeing you every day brought me physical pain. The "snapshot" that is most firm in this memory, is of you leaving the room. You looked back over your shoulder and looked at me. At least, I like to tell myself you were looking at me. Perhaps you were just taking in the scene one last time, to make a memory. But for a moment, our eyes met and we were together. It was the highlight of my night... Well, except for seeing your legs in those heels. Not many things could have topped that... only you leaving with me, THAT would have been the trump card to the whole prom. If only we could go back...

Missing you

I could not believe that such detail was burned into his memory. I was touched and flattered. I thought it was funny that he kept referring to his "date," and then it dawned on me that, most likely, he had no clue of what her name had been. And that thought made me smile and a tiny giggle came to the surface. It was getting easier to giggle, the emptier the wine bottle got. I wonder why that was?

The next few entries were just the normal "touching base" variety, and then one that, again, stole my heart. The girls and I had done a family photo shoot and I posted my favorite pictures from it. Most of my favorites were candid shots the photographer had taken when the girls and I were completely unaware he was taking them. Jack had copied every one of those pictures into this email and shared under each what he saw in it.

SWOON

There were like... over 30 of them. I wondered how much time he had spent looking at them and how often he still went back to them. My favorite one of just the girls was mostly a headshot of them with their heads tilted together. He commented, "They look so much like you at that age." I never thought that. To me, they were Brad, made-over, only with my eyes. Maybe it was because I WANTED to see Brad in them. I didn't see myself, or hold myself in the same esteem, as others seemed to. I definitely never thought of myself as beautiful, but my girls were exactly that. They were beautiful from their insides out. They were everything that I always wanted to be when I was their age: confident, talented, smart, funny, and pretty. And thanks to ten grand spent at the orthodontist, they had perfect teeth. They were the complete package, and I felt so blessed to be their mom.

The next email waiting in the queue… made my "radar" go off, and my hair stand on end. A weird feeling came with reading it. The entry just seemed odd to me, like a piece of a puzzle that's in the wrong box, but you're not quite sure where its true home is, so you don't know what to do with it at that moment.

Sunshine,

Something is going on here. I'm working on figure out exactly what it is. But she has been coming home late (which has, actually, been nice. Now I don't have to find reasons to stay gone all the time and I can enjoy being here), and she is always in a good mood, it seems. This is STRANGE behavior for her so I'm keeping my guard up as I learned a long time ago not to trust her any farther than I could throw her. And she's become a pretty big gal, so that would not be far at all. I'm a little scared to eat anything she prepares, HA!! I'm just kidding, seriously, I doubt that she's trying to kill me, too many people know too much about our history and she's smart enough to know she would get caught. I'm just not sure what she's up to... But she is definitely up to something.

All my love

I was relieved that I had read this after laying eyes on him. Even him joking about her killing him, creeped me out and made me furious! They must have really had some whoppers for fights, I was guessing. Had their kids grown up with them being hateful to each other? I just couldn't imagine Jack being hateful, especially to a woman. He had always been such a gentleman. The vision of her in my head, and the thought of her treating him ugly, made my cheeks flush with anger. I'm sure the wine had a role in my overreaction, but I was thoroughly angry, nonetheless. I closed the finished entry, moved on to the next, and continued in that pattern until the wine bottle was empty, and sleep crept over me in my numb, alcohol-induced state.

I fell asleep hard and deep. My comfy chair had a history of lulling me into sound, restful sleep, and it was tag-teaming with the entire bottle of wine I'd managed to knock out, alone.

12

THE REPLAY

It wasn't long before I was completely asleep and dreaming. Naturally, I would dream of him. There was nothing else weighing on my mind that could press its way into my subconscious. He had been in my every thought for over 24 hours, so I had to see it coming. Again, I was back in a memory, my best memory, the night he had finally made love to me.

Nothing ever changed when I relived this memory in a dream. It played the same as it would if it were burned onto a DVD, and our images so vivid, it would have to be a Blu-ray, playing on the most up-to-date HDTV available. There was no fuzziness to this memory, it had remained crystal clear all these years. Perhaps, because I had returned to it so frequently for comfort over the years, it had never had the opportunity to fade. It all played again for the seventy-three thousandth time, him coming in the door, kissing me, running his fingers through my hair. My hands running over his perfect body, discovering and appreciating each perfect muscle. I again felt our smooth, soft landing onto the bed and him turning the tables to pull me on top of him, after I had silently begged him to give me a moment to recover from him touching me intimately, for the first time.

As I was now straddling him, I felt more in control of how fast we were to progress. I wanted this to last forever, and from his responses, I gathered he felt the same way. He was patient with me, never forcing, or pushing limits as I set them. I pressed our chests together and returned my mouth to his... sweetness. His kisses were perfect, not too wet or fast, but gentle and almost teasing. And so soft, not so firm that I felt I had to apply back pressure to keep my head straight. Our tongues lightly brushing against the other's and teasingly against the other's lips. I lightly bit his bottom lip and paused for a moment to gently suck on it, before I continued kissing down to his chin and on to his throat. It all was so natural between us, effortless... perfect. After many kisses to his mouth, face, neck, and oh, the earlobes, ya can't forget the earlobes, and having my fingers all knotted in his hair... I wanted to feel him closer to me. I began to rise up; with my hands under his arms, I scooped him up by his shoulders and gently urged him to sit up with me. As soon as his back was clear of the bed, I found the bottom of his T-shirt and lifted it up over his head. The sight of his perfect chest, softly illuminated by the light coming through the open bedroom door, took my breath away. I pushed him back onto the bed and let myself fall with him. His hand, yes, just one hand, was immediately running up my back under my shirt and "snap" there went my bra clasps. I thought to myself, *One-handed, that quick?? Damn, he's good*. I raised myself up just enough to grab the base of my shirt and remove it over my head, bra and all, and tossed it off the bed without hitting him in the face. Then I immediately returned my bare chest to his, longing to finally feel the heat from his skin on mine.

His hands were so strong, soft, and warm as he wrapped his arms around me and caressed my back. He pulled me in tighter to him, as he kissed my mouth and neck. We were lying crossways on the bed, and as I realized that I was now half naked, I became very conscious of my body. I had grown heavy and was embarrassed by my flab... I made an excuse of being cold, so we could move, and I could hide myself under the covers, away from his beautiful eyes. After making my claim to being cold, I quickly relocated to the "normal" position one takes in a bed and covered most of me. Somehow, I managed to miss my left breast. The sheet was lying perfectly down the middle of my chest, then across to my left hip. As he began to make his move to join me, he crawled, catlike, on all fours, hovering over me. He stopped at my exposed breast like he had stumbled onto a treasure, and he scooped it up lightly, caressing it with his right hand, so very gently, then he bent his head down slowly and touched my nipple with only his tongue, causing an electric current to course through my entire body. He was so tender, his tongue so gentle, that it felt how I can only imagine it would feel to be touched by a whisper. He then took it into his mouth and sweetly sucked on it, in between kissing the entire exposed area. I was covered in goose bumps. Every nerve ending was on high alert, and my heart continued to pound uncontrollably. So much for me being in control of the encounter, I was putty in his gentle hands.

I encouraged him to join me lying properly, head on pillows, he complied and made the move to rest on his back to my left-hand side. I immediately rolled to my side and began kissing his perfect chest... then down to his stomach, and on to the waist of his jeans. I took the corner of the button hole and began to pull, one-handed, to free the button. I slowly unzipped the zipper and followed the newly created opening, with my kisses. I gently tugged downward, and his hands returned to assist in removing his jeans, revealing his green-and-blue-plaid boxers, sexy. I don't know why, but I have always preferred boxers to briefs. He tossed his jeans to the floor at the foot of the bed, in a move that resembled someone shooting a free-throw shot during a basketball game. I returned my attention to his boxers as soon as I heard his jeans hit the floor, and his right arm returned to rest around me. I was in control again; total control.

I gently pulled the elastic up off his stomach, only to pull it down, and over the object I was in search of. With his help, I managed to pull his boxers down below his hip bones, then slowly brought my hand back to my prize; letting just my fingertips graze his skin. It was waiting there... hard, pulsing, and begging for attention. I took him gently into my hand, causing him to inhale sharply at my touch. Then, wrapping my fingers firmly around the middle of the shaft, I guided the head to rest softly on my bottom lip, as I slowly used my tongue to trace its outline.

"Oh my God..." he said, in a tone that made me wonder if this was his first oral experience. Good, I was pleasing him. I couldn't help but let a small grin escape, as I decided to see how far I could push him. I moved my mouth to the base and, again slowly and gently, ran my tongue lightly from the base slowly up the center line, straight through the heart-shaped joining near the top of the head, then tracing it again.

"OH MY GOD..."

I had him, another brief grin surfaced on my mouth. I turned to face him and admitted, "I have a little hidden talent." A talent that he had been unaware of.) He agreed.

As I returned my focus to seeing how wild I could drive him, he began tugging at the waist of my jeans and trying to reach down into them, which was an impossible task with me bent and my knees curled up. "Take these off, I HAVE to touch you..." he said, as I began my first full descent, taking him fully into my mouth. His entire body went rigid with pleasure, as he took in a deep breath and held it. I was really enjoying having him under my control. I had waited for years for this opportunity; the chance to make him want me more than he could have ever imagined possible. After rolling my tongue around a few more times, with the head still in my mouth, I could tell he needed a moment to calm down, before an unwelcomed premature ending to our encounter occurred, so I relented and lay back to remove my jeans for him, while I let him regain control and his focus.

"Did you say you wanted these off?" I asked in a sweet, slightly teasing tone.

"Yeah," he replied in a soft, out-of-breath exhale.

Right where I want you, I thought to myself. Muwahahahahaha… I tossed my jeans to the floor at the foot of the bed, and then removed my socks, just because. I rolled slowly, completely naked now, returning to my post, and started back where I had left off. He began intimately exploring me… trying to use his fingers to return the pleasure I was supplying him. After a few moments, he had to abandon his effort, as touching me during his heightened sense of excitement was leading him very close to his own undoing. He had to lie back and focus on keeping it together. I wondered what he was thinking of, to keep himself semi-detached from the moment, as I made my move again, all the way down. This time, I kept going until he was past the back of my throat, and there was no more of him left to take in…

"OH, HONEY…"

If my mouth hadn't been full, I would have giggled… He was mine. I was having my way with him, and he was all but helpless in my hands. I saw his left hand appear in my peripheral vision, at the same moment that I noticed that his balls had retreated up into his body… the first sign that the end is near.

"Come up here so I can hold you…" he urgently requested.

I realized his hand had appeared as backup, in case he had to insist and assist in my departure… He was at his limit and didn't want things to end here. I smiled to myself again and thought, *Okay, this time I'll let you off easy,* as I slowly kissed my way back up, first kissing his hip bone, as my hand stopped its gentle up-and-down motion, then slowly, reluctantly releasing him. His tense frame relaxed minutely, as I heard him take in another deep, calming breath.

I kissed up his side, his right arm still around me, and his left hand now combing through my hair. My last kiss landing on his chest, just below his nipple, I looked up and met his bright eyes, as I made my soft request.

"Make love to me."

He responded with, "Are you sure?"

I was not surprised, always the gentleman, he wanted to be sure I would have no regrets. I was way more than sure, it was safe to say that I had never been more certain of any decision in my entire life... I wanted him. I wanted to be one with him, more than anything I had ever wanted before. The response I chose was an effort to return his considerate question.

"Are you?"

He, without hesitation, replied, "Yeah."

That was it, it was on. Still having his right arm behind me, he scooped me up and rolled to be on top of me. My legs had spread during the movement and we landed in perfect missionary position. He looked deep into my eyes, so deep that our souls met, as he entered me in one gentle, smooth thrust. I took in a quick deep breath, as he immediately was as deep as I could take him. The emotion of finally being in this moment with him, combined with how perfectly we fit together, led to my almost instantaneous climax. My eyes closed as they rolled to the back of my head, in a moment of complete surrender and ecstasy. The warm wetness that followed was insane. How was it possible for me to be any more aroused?

His slow, gentle, rhythmic motion never slowed. He bent down until his lips brushed against my ear as he said softly, "You feel so good..."

That was an understatement for how he felt to me. I responded with my initial observation.

"I always knew we would fit perfectly together."

He sighed contently in agreement, "Mmmmm…"

He continued his perfect rhythm, only retracting slightly, staying as deep inside me as I could take, like he wanted to stay joined as much as possible. I was in complete agreement with this intention. My hips were raised up off the bed, trying to keep me as close to him as humanly possible, and matching his motions. We moved rhythmically together, as one perfect body. My legs wrapped around his in a lock as strong as steel. Not long after our brief exchange his voice returned… shaky and a bit breathless, with the announcement that he could no longer hold off the inevitable. I was unable to respond, as I was right there with him, at the height of excitement and pleasure, my voice failed me. He quit any signs of reverse motion, only pushing more forward. He again met my eyes and looked intently into them, as he was again as deep as he could possibly go, he locked onto my gaze, and I felt him explode. I joined him for my second full orgasm. He came intense and hard, as if releasing all the years of waiting for the opportunity; then he relaxed and took in a deep cleansing breath.

The lull only lasted a brief moment, as he returned to his gentle soft rhythm. His hardness never fading, *Oh wow!* I thought to myself… *he's not finished!* He continued in his quest to please me. Did he not realize that he had already brought me to orgasm twice? He had control now, and was seeing how wild he could drive me, I guessed. And his quest succeeded, I was helpless. Just as I was as aroused as I could possibly be, goose bumps on my goose bumps on top of my goose bumps, he brought me to full climax for the third time. Afraid that he would feel my shiver, I managed to voice, "It's okay, it's okay." As my body relaxed, I noticed that his body was covered in a thin layer of sweat now, glistening in the pale light, and I appreciated the beautiful perfection hovering over me.

He scooped me up against him with his left arm and rolled to my left. We moved perfectly as one body and when we rested in our new position I was on top of him, and he remained inside of me. Another confirmation of how we were made to fit together. He released me as we landed, and the sweetest smile appeared on his face. I ran my hands up his outstretched arms, his left one curved above his head, and his right was straight out, lying across my side of the bed; I knotted my fingers with his. I continued our rhythmic motion ever so slightly, as I seriously was beyond my point of highest sensitivity. My system was at risk of being at overload status, with every hair on my body standing up, making every touch feel electric, every tiny movement felt like a landslide, and I was concerned I might faint, I was so lightheaded. I slowed to a stop, keeping him inside me as I kissed his chin and his neck, enjoying the euphoria pulsing through my entire body. I finally lifted myself free of him, nestling myself beside him with my head on his chest... heaven. He held me, gently stroking my back and covering the hand I had rested on his chest, with his other hand. After a few minutes, he squeezed my hand and expressed his need to use the shower. Kissing the top of my head, he left me wrapped in the sheets and afterglow.

This was the one moment in my entire life that I could truly say I felt complete. I had almost fallen asleep, enjoying my deep contented feeling, when he returned to say goodbye. With all contentment gone... immediately, the feeling was replaced by shock and panic that surged through me so quick that I felt dizzy. Full body sobs made their exit and tears started to flow. He had looked distraught and beaten, like leaving me was the very last thing he wanted to do but had no choice. My tears were breaking his heart; he'd never seen me cry over him, so this was new to him. He looked mortified, as if causing me this much pain was physically painful and unbearable to him. He kissed my cheek, turned, and walked out. The wail that left my body surprised even me… and as it had in the past, so many times, it woke me. It woke me, because I cried out in my sleep as well… again.

I opened my eyes, "Separate Ways" was playing; the perfect song to accompany the remainder of the memory, as I allowed it to play out in my mind. I had jumped out of the bed, wrapped in just the sheet and hurried to the door, calling after him. He was nowhere to be seen in the hallway. I closed the door and half ran to the bedroom window. There he was, exiting the building, walking to the parking lot. He went straight to his truck, got in, and pulled out, never looking back. I was standing holding the sheet together with one hand, with the other pressed flat on the window above my head. I sobbed and slid down the length of the window into a ball on the floor, after I watched his taillights fade out of view. **He never looked back**.

13

AWAKENING

The memory left me feeling numb, as it always did. Not angry or hurt, just numb and empty. As the sleepy fog cleared from my head, I opened my eyes to discover that the pale light of dawn was only just beginning to seep into the room from behind the closed blinds.

Journey was still singing when I became aware that my head was killing me. An entire bottle of wine… what had I been thinking? *OUCH.* I threw the throw off me and stretched, then got up and headed to the bathroom to pee and find some ibuprofen. I flipped on the light and glanced in the mirror… oh yeah, his shirt. My hair was at an insane level of disheveled. I took care of my pressing need to pee, then grabbed a bottle of relief from the medicine cabinet and made way for the kitchen. It was almost 7 a.m. I made a mental note that I would need a nap, later.

I took the medicine while my coffee was filling up in my mug, then grabbed it and went to check my phone. It was dead, after two nights of forgetting to plug it in, whoops. I took it over to my desk and plugged it in. It was so dead, it would be a few minutes before it would respond to anything, so I walked over to where my laptop had landed for the night. Luckily, I had left it plugged in, knowing that I would have it humming for an extended session, yesterday. I opened it to discover multiple new emails, all arriving after I had passed out... which had been rather early, compared to the night before. I tried to think of the last time I recalled seeing... 10:45 maybe? I hadn't logged out, so I had appeared active all-night long. 11:10 was his first attempt.

> Hey, Sunshine... feel like talking yet?

Then 11:20:

> Hello? Are you there?

11:30

> You're worrying me, we don't have to talk, but please answer me...

11:35

> Your phone is going straight to voicemail... If you don't answer me by midnight, I'm coming over there. Please let me know you're okay.

11:50

> I can't stand it, I'm heading that way, I have to know you're okay.

12:30

> You didn't answer when I knocked, so I peeped through the blinds and

was relieved to see you passed out with the empty wine bottle on the table beside you. Thank God your neighbors didn't see me and call the cops. You scared the hell out of me. I thought maybe I had pushed you too far, and you had done something desperate or made a run for it. Or, someone had broken in and hurt you! Yes, my imagination got away from me. I'm going to bed, now that I know you are safe. Please call me in the morning.

I love you, with all of me…

Oh, my cheese!! He was crazy! I didn't feel like getting up to retrieve my phone and have to move the charger and all, so I just opened a new email to send him a message.

YOU ARE SUCH A GOOBER. Why would you think I would hurt myself over you, NOW? I'm sorry to tell ya, but you missed that stage many years ago. You are beyond insane. My phone is dead and charging, so don't bother trying to call.

I couldn't remember where I had left off in his "journal," wow, that wine had been good. As I quickly scrolled back through, glancing at subjects, or the first few lines, if no subject was provided, there were only a few that had been opened, that I had no clear memory of reading, and had to read again. There were only a couple hundred left. I had been almost done when I fell asleep. *Crap*! If I hadn't passed out, I probably would have finished last night! However, I would have had to read them all again, sober, to know what they contained. That jackass and his wine delivery service, sigh. My heart still felt heavy with the remnants of my recurring dream still floating through my subconscious. I wondered if he ever thought back on that night or had any detailed memory of it all. Probably not, guys were different. But who knew, he had already surprised me several times with his recall… maybe he did. I had reached the more current portion of his entries, and the next one I opened was news of the divorce.

My Sunshine,

I get to write today, with no fear of being discovered or accused, and with joy in my soul. She informed me last night that she has been having an affair, and she wants a divorce. Relief has washed over me, in a way I can only assume a man pardoned from death row would feel. I know that's an over exaggeration, but it's the best I have, to describe how I'm feeling.

The light in my heart that comes with knowing that I only have a few months left before I can see you, is so bright, I'm sure it's visible from space! And I make this promise to you here, now. The MOMENT that I'm free, I am running to you and praying you will have me.

Once again, and FINALLY, yours only

Holy shit!! After all her ugly accusations to me, her holier-than-thou attitude all those years ago, she went and messed around on him! *WOW*!! I was speechless. I had *not* seen that one coming. An eventual, mutual, "we're done here, please kiss my ass," sure… But SHE had an affair AND left for it. I was going to have to get some more coffee in me, and then make sure I had read that right. Then I would have to call Faith and Margo, they were gonna plotz! I had made jokes for years, about hoping she would get a boyfriend and run away with him. Were they jokes or wishes? To be honest, that scenario had been one of the deepest desires of my heart. And I'll be damned, it had happened! I followed through with my plan and drank about half of my coffee before I began to read that one again from the top. Yep, I had read every word right. And I noted that it was dated almost 7 months ago. Had he really run to me the moment he was clear of her? My heart skipped a beat as I let that sink in.

In the following emails, with the exception of how the divorce was progressing, he never mentioned her again. And his entries became regular… daily, more often than not. His favorite subject in the most recent ones was only his impatience with the wait to see me and hold me. These were all VERY different from the previous, completely platonic communications. In one, he caught me off guard with a steamy entry, when he had let his imagination run with the other things he hoped to be doing with me very soon… tender things, sexy things… naughty things. That one gave me goose bumps and it was like reading a classy dirty novel. I guess he did remember a lot of the details of our one night together, as he used the word "again" several times throughout the fantasy. I felt like I needed a cold shower after reading that one. Just for fun, I read it again, too. Okay, okay, so I read it like twelve more times… Who wouldn't?

The very last one, dated the afternoon of his first call to me, would forever be burned in my heart. Even if I were to walk away from him forever, his words had struck hard and deep, in a way that I would never be able to erase; like an engraving in stone.

My Sunshine,

I have just settled into my hotel room, here in your world. It's beautiful here—I can see why you didn't return home after Brad died. The people have already made an impression on me with their friendliness, they have been so helpful and kind. I had no problem finding your house, thanks to their directions, as my GPS is crap and seems to have a mind of its own. I wasn't surprised to find that your house is beautiful, with so many flowers and trees in the yard, welcoming any who may wander up the front walk.

I was lucky enough to get to see you for a few brief moments, as you and the girls walked out to the mailbox before getting in the truck to leave. Watching you laugh together and seeing the joy on your face when you were simply looking at them... lit up my soul. It also brought fear back into my heart. My goal in coming here is to bring you back home with me, at least, as soon as the girls have finished high school. But for the first time, it strikes me that this has become your home now.

With that being acknowledged, I've made a decision. If my getting to live the rest of my life with you requires that I leave everything behind to come here, then that's what I will do. I've said many times in these past letters that your happiness is all that is important, and now I must prove it. I cannot be happy without you, and therefore, I will be wherever you are.

My hands are beginning to shake now, from nervous excitement so I must end here, so that I can make the call that I have longed to make for so many long years. I think I may be more nervous now than I was with my first call to you in high school! My nerves are flying and taking my emotions with them. I will hear your sweet, perfect voice soon. Even if you tell me to kiss your ass, which I pray is NOT the case, it will be the sweetest sounding command I've ever been given. My prayer is to have my arms around you in only a few hours, and that you will be reading this, soon after.

With more love than you know

Tears filled my eyes, as I realized the depth of his love for me. He was willing to leave his life behind to come and make a new one with me. That was huge. Funny, in all my dreams previous to his arrival, and the moments since our reunion, that I had actually tried to consider us being together, I had never gone as far as to wonder **where** we would spend this "forever" together. I guess I had always pushed it to the back of my mind as a trivial detail, because all that mattered was being with him. But now that the subject was open, this was anything but trivial; it was a very big deal. Where did I want to be? My girls, of course, had their lives here for the next two years, but after that, who knew where they would end up? But having someone tell you that they will give up everything for you… that's deep, and a definite game changer.

Was it crazy that I could make the same offer to him? Again, all my heart cared about was being with him, forever. I knew, without a doubt, that my girls would always come to see me wherever I was, and vice versa. At some point, the cord is cut, and you are no longer solely revolving around the lives of your children. If your kids are 40, and you are still joined at the hip… it's kinda creepy in a Bates Motel kind of way. Was I settled, then? Had I made my decision to forgive his absence and trust him not to ever hurt me again? It was definitely time to call Faith and Margo and catch them up. They were gonna kill me for calling at this ungodly hour, as they were an hour behind me in their time zone, but I was at a crossroad and needed some unbiased direction. I got up and went to the desk to use my phone, since it was still charging.

14

DELIBERATIONS

"Hello…" Margo's voice sounded raspy and confused with just a hint of pissed.

"Hey, it's me. Sorry, but I need you to wake up, shit just got real. Hold on while I try to get Faith on." Faith had sounded almost the same, only not pissed but concerned, her experience with early calls was that someone was dead.

When I switched back to Margo, her first words were, "What the hell, woman!? It's SEVEN freakin' THIRTY on a SUNDAY! This had better be good, did you get laid?"

Faith responded, "Oh my goodness… wait… did you?"

I had to laugh out loud as I replied, "NO… get your minds out of the gutter and try to focus with me for a minute, please."

"Okay," replied Margo, "listening."

Faith yawned as she added, "Me too."

First, I shared some of the emails I had read in my drunkenness, then how he had freaked when I didn't respond, as I had passed out after drinking an entire bottle of wine, alone. Margo shot in a, "That's our girl!" Faith and I laughed. I went on to share my response to him this morning, just to insure they were fully awake, when I dropped the bomb.

"She had an affair and left him," I said matter-of-factly.

"SHUT UP!!" Faith exclaimed, in disbelief.

Margo was almost on top of her, with, "GET OUT!!"

"Yep, that's what happened, Mrs. 'how dare you talk to my husband' got her some on the side and liked it. So, she is totally gone, by her choice."

Faith asked, "Did he say how long they've been divorced?"

"Separated about seven months, the process was ugly, but it was just final, five days ago." Just enough time, I thought to myself, for him to get things settled, then arrange things to be covered at work, before he headed out. Not exactly "the moment" but less than a week, not too shabby.

"Alrighty, then," replied Margo, "so that has to change things for you."

"Hold on," I answered, "I haven't even gotten to the shocking part yet." I then relayed the last letter. As I read the pledge of his devotion, it spoke again to my heart, as I shared his intention, his promise to me, with them. I received silence from the other ends of the call. "Well don't be shy now, you two!! What do I do??"

Faith responded, "What does your heart tell you?"

"My heart would have married him yesterday, Fay. It's my mind that's hung up, I think. I'm so scared to trust him again. I really don't think I could live through losing him again. It came so close to killing me last time, I don't think I have it in me to fight it again."

"You're stronger than you think you are," replied Margo, "and my gut is telling me that it's not anything to be concerned about. I feel like the universe has finally righted a wrong, and all will be well, now." Margo could be such a "make love, not war" hippie, and I loved that about her. But don't you dare let her catch a milk jug in your trash, she'd take your head off for not recycling.

However, Faith agreed with her. "I agree. I sense peace."

The weirdest part was, so did I, it was just that I was scared to death to accept it. I didn't feel like I deserved it.

"Well, okay... I'm thinking of calling him and asking him to come over to talk... what do y'all think?"

"I think it's time, and I think you're ready," Faith said.

Margo agreed and added, "And maybe you'll get some. HA!"

"Oh my word," I said over them both, laughing. "I'll talk to y'all later, BYE!" I hung up, without listening for their goodbyes. Sex was the LAST thing I needed to have on my mind. I needed a clear, focused head before I made my next call... to him. My heart started skipping like it was headed for a playground, as "Need You Now" started playing in the background.

I sat and finished my coffee with no thoughts running through my head, at all. I just focused on the warmth of the liquid soothing my headache, and then completely zoned out for a bit after my cup was empty and simply sat there, content, in the quiet calm. When the caffeine kicked in, I noticed it was almost ten, I needed to make this call. I hoped he was up... I took a deep cleansing breath to calm my nerves and realized, like him, I doubted I had ever been more nervous about calling him, even in high school. I brought up the recent calls log and touched his name... no backing out like the good ole days... it was done and ringing already. He answered so quickly, it surprised me.

"Good morning, my love, how did you sleep?"

His voice washed over me like a warm shower, causing me to momentarily lose my train of thought. After a few seconds of silence, he added, "You okay, Sunshine?" to his original question.

I regained my senses but stuttered my reply. "Yeah, I... I'm okay, how are you?"

"I'm talking to the woman I love, so I've never been better!"

His voice sounded like that of a five-year-old child waiting in line to see Santa. He truly was thrilled that I was FINALLY calling. Again, he spoke. "I would love to take you to breakfast."

"Ugh, food... no, thank you," I responded. My head had just started to ease a bit, but my stomach was not on board with welcoming food yet.

"Oh right... the empty bottle of wine."

"Shhhhh, don't speak of it."

He chuckled softly, and my heart raced, I would never tire of that sound.

"I did call to ask for a favor, though."

"Absolutely anything your heart desires, will be my pleasure."

I thought to myself, *turn it down a notch... this may not go the way you're hoping.*

"Would you come over, please? I'd like to talk, ask some questions, and try to get some stuff straight and settled in my mind."

He answered almost immediately, "Sure. Let me shower, then I'm on my way. Can I stop and get you anything, DONUTS maybe?"

"UGH..."

"Oh sorry, my bad." And he chuckled again. "I'll be right there, Sunshine."

"Don't rush. I'll be here."

"About forty-five minutes?"

"Okay. Thank you, bye..."

I hung up without waiting for a farewell from him. He still remembered that I love donuts.

SWOON

I considered taking a shower too, then thought *nope, let him embrace the funk.* However, not wanting to appear completely unkempt and gross, I did brush my teeth, ran a brush through my unruly hair and put it up in a loose bun. Before leaving the bathroom, I decided to add a tad of fragrance with one of my favorite essential oil blends, just in case I did happen to smell funky, which I shouldn't, seeing how I had just sat still in the same chair for most of the last 24 hours, but one can't be too careful when it comes to body odor, in my opinion. He was going to see the real me again today. No makeup, sweats, and bare feet. Love it or leave it.

It was getting close to eleven. The girls weren't coming home until after dinner. This one weekend a month was a ritual with Brad's parents since his death, so I knew with certainty that they would pull up at eight o'clock this evening like clockwork, or I would get a call to inform me that they had made a stop for ice cream and would be a bit tardy. His parents had always been sensitive to the fact that after what had happened to Brad, I would easily freak out, if they were late with the girls without calling. They were really good people, and they were so proud of their granddaughters. They had been a blessing to our lives, and I was glad that the girls were close to them.

As I was in the process of being thankful again, for the girls being away for this emotionally taxing weekend, I found it odd that he had managed to appear on the single weekend in the month that was scheduled for my girls to spend away from home. Which reminded me of the question: where was he getting his information? Sure, Facebook had provided a window to some things, but I had never been public with my girls' lives, or schedules, for their safety. I had a feeling that there was a spy somewhere… but who? It had to be one of our classmates; thanks to social media, a large number of us were now in easy contact with each other. But who was close enough to have this detailed information, yet not close enough for me to immediately suspect them? Perhaps I was wrong, and his arrival had just been a lucky coincidence? My gut feeling was that it was not; another question to add to my list.

I had just set my second cup of coffee beside my big chair, when he knocked. My heart stopped briefly, then began to race. I had no idea where this was going to lead. With only two options, accepting his offer, or telling him to go, one would think I would have an inclination to one or the other. But, my overjoyed heart and my self-preservation-focused mind were still at war. I had no idea why I had asked him over, other than I just wanted to see him again, spend time just being with him… it had always come so naturally for us. I closed my eyes and took a deep breath and walked to the door. I opened it slowly, trying to slow my heart down before actually laying eyes on him, as I knew it was only going to speed up more, when I saw him. He was standing there, with his hands in the pockets of his stylish jeans, that were purposely and strategically ripped up, and a simple sky-blue T-shirt that made his eyes stand out even more so than normal.

SWOON

I wanted to melt into his arms, with every fiber of my being, but my mind recovered just in time and shouted, *Whoa, girl, steady now.* I managed to say, "Hey," as I stepped back to make room for him to enter.

"Hey, Sunshine, you look beautiful for being hungover. And you're still rockin' my stolen shirt, I see." He leaned down and softly kissed my forehead.

"Thanks."

The brief touch of his lips on my skin flowed down through me like the first, sweet sip of hot chocolate on a cold night; bringing with it a sense of peace, perfect calm, and a flush to my cheeks. I motioned to the furniture, and he sat in the middle of the sofa. I knew he was hoping that I would join him there, and it would leave no space between us. He would be disappointed.

"Would you like some coffee?" I offered.

"That would be great, thanks."

"Just black, if I remember correctly…"

"Your memory is perfect."

I turned and went to the kitchen, when I returned, he was waiting, sitting on the edge of the sofa, his legs apart, elbows resting on his knees and his hands locked together between his knees, by intertwined fingers. He looked up when I re-entered the room, with a look that made me momentarily pause to try and assign an emotion to it. Even though he was lovingly smiling at me, his eyes were expressing something more… pain… or fear, maybe?

That was it, it was fear. My heart physically ached, to see that look in those precious eyes. They became even more apprehensive when I handed him his coffee, then turned to go sit in my big chair, instead of taking a spot next to him on the sofa. I felt bad for him. He looked pitiful, so I spoke first.

"You okay?"

He took a sip of coffee, then set it down on the coffee table as he nodded and replied. "Yeah, yeah, I'm great."

But his voice trailed off as he said it, and his gaze lingered on his cup, obvious signs that he was lying. I tilted my head and held my gaze on him, until my silence caused him to return his attention to me. I focused my eyes on his. When his eyes finally met mine, I raised my brow in a silent question of doubt. He looked away, licked his lips then rubbed them together, before he gently sank his teeth into the bottom one.

He finally responded, "Okay, no. I'm a wreck, actually. Not knowing what you're thinking is pure hell. And I'm terrified of losing you again knowing this time would be forever."

I had to empathetically respond, I had been there. Actually, I had lived there. It was a scary, lonely place, and I wouldn't want anyone to be stuck there for a moment, much less the lifetime I had spent in that feeling.

"Welcome to my world. I completely understand what you're feeling, and I'm sorry that you find yourself there.

I'm hoping that we will have everything settled one way or the other, just as soon as possible... living in this emotional hell isn't exactly a picnic for me either. However, it's not my intention to make that decision today." He returned his eyes to mine, and I gave him an understanding half smile as I continued. "If that helps you to calm down and feel better."

He just nodded reassuringly and replied, "It helps a little bit, not as much as 'I love you and I want to be with you forever.' It WOULD help if I heard you say that."

He cocked his head, shooting me a quick wink, knowing that was not to be my response in this moment.

"That being understood, I guess I should start," I said.

"Okay, what can I answer for you?"

I took a deep breath and proceeded with my first question.

"We might as well start at the beginning. Why didn't you just tell me how you felt before we graduated... and got this so screwed up?"

Crap, the tears were back. I fought successfully to keep them in my eyes and not let them stream out. I had decided to leave my music on before he arrived, and now Journey had joined our conversation, playing "Faithfully" softly in the background. He noticed too, as his eyes left mine and flashed to the TV screen for only a moment, a smile crossing his lips. Then he swallowed hard and returned his attention to me.

"I could ask you the same question, but for my side, it's simple, because I was a coward and couldn't swallow my pride to tell you. I was afraid you didn't feel the same way, and I would look like an idiot in front of you. I should have manned up and come for you, so many times over the years, before the possibility of success had become impossible. And I regret that, more that I could ever put into words."

I had to respond, it wasn't entirely all his fault... He was right. I, too, had a voice that I had chosen not to use.

"You're right, I'm to blame too. I could have spoken up so many times, but I was so scared of being rejected that I just couldn't make myself tell you."

His eyes sparked at my confession, and he replied so softly it was almost a whisper.

"If I had even minutely thought that you felt that way, I would have been all over the opportunity to be yours again." And he smiled a wishful smile, for a time long gone.

"I agree. I would have married you before our caps hit the ground, if you'd asked me at graduation."

I smiled as sweetly as I ever had at him, with the memory of our class in a circle throwing our caps in the air in celebration.

"Okay, so if you had these undying feelings for me, how could you marry *her*?"

My voice broke with the hurt and pain that the thought of his marriage had always caused me. Luckily, enough anger accompanied the feelings that I was able to keep the mounting tears in check. He raised his eyebrows and shoulders simultaneously, as he shook his head slightly.

"I had lost touch with you and assumed you were gone forever, and that you never gave me a second thought. I tried to move on, and honestly, I rushed into it. When you surfaced right before the wedding, I had never been happier to see anyone in my entire life, yet completely devastated at the same time. I've always tried to be a man of my word, so I knew I had no choice but to go ahead with the wedding, as planned. I just prayed that you would find someone who would adore you as much as I did, and that he would give you the life you deserved. Even though the thought of another man made me sick inside, it meant more to me that you be happy."

His eyes said that he needed assurance that his sacrifice had not been in vain, so I complied.

"I did have that for a time, if knowing that helps you feel better. I was content. Not as happy as I probably could have been, but in no way did I suffer. He was good to me, a devoted husband and father. When he died, I accepted that God knew I didn't deserve him, 'cause I had never shared the secret that I hid in my heart, with him, that he wasn't my only love, and that I could never love him the way I did you. That part of my soul was with you forever... so God took him away from me."

"Oh, Sunshine... It was just an accident, God wasn't punishing you..."

"Yeah, well... it felt like punishment. And I took it, knowing I had not done Brad right, by keeping my feelings a secret."

I had never voiced that to anyone, and it felt good to get it out. I could tell him anything, except that I still loved him, it had been that way since the moment we broke up when I was 16; pure insanity in its simplest form. I continued with a follow-up question.

"If you knew that you weren't going to call it off, why did you come to me? I thought I had won, that the nightmare was finally over; that you had chosen ME and we were going to be together! Knowing what I know now... that was kind of cruel, don't you think?"

He stared at me blankly. Only, in his eyes, I could see that he was desperately searching for the right words. After a very long, silent minute he finally spoke. "There's no excuse good enough to explain that away... pure and simple, I was being completely selfish."

I glared at him now, hurt and anger boiling near the surface. I couldn't speak, and the color drained from my face. I felt sick. Seeing the distress wash over me, he was immediately on his feet and he came and knelt on one knee in front of me, taking my face into his strong hands.

"I'm so very sorry... I... I just couldn't fight the urge to see you. I really went with the intention of us just spending some time together... just talking. I did NOT go there with the motive of making love to you... please believe me!"

The tears wouldn't stay put any longer, and they flowed freely from my eyes, down my cheeks and over his hands. He tried to wipe them away with his thumbs, but there were too many. There was a constant stream flowing down my face, originating from deep in my heart. He slowly dropped his hands as he leaned in to wrap his arms around me. He pulled me in until my head came to rest on his right shoulder, my face snuggled up against his neck and my lips touching just above his collarbone. My quiet tears became sobs. He began to slowly rock from side to side, stroking my hair, as I released a lifetime of regret, hurt, and pain, fully in front of him, for the very first time. My unspoken love, my overwhelming sense of abandonment, my grief at Brad's death, the struggle of being a single parent, everything... all my life's struggles and regrets made their full exit in the safety of his embrace.

He was silent, but I realized that he was crying too, as his tears were mingling with mine. I could feel them when they ran from his cheek onto my face. We seemed to stay like that forever, frozen in a bond of emotional surrender. As I regained some composure, I took a deep breath and slowly pulled back. He relented in his embrace, but again took my face into his hands. He looked deeply and sincerely into my eyes.

"Leaving you that night was the hardest thing I've ever done. And I never wanted to see you cry like that again... and now look what's happened, look at what I've done." He again used his thumbs, and this time, was successful in clearing the tears away from my cheeks.

He sweetly smiled at me, saying, "That's better... no more tears, my Sunshine.

Everything is going to be okay, and I promise that it will be my life's ambition to never hurt you to tears again. Ever."

Raising my hands, I dried his cheeks as well, then returned them to my lap. We stayed locked in each other's eyes for a few moments, before he leaned in and slowly and gently placed his mouth on mine... as softly and tenderly as a first kiss, as if he was unsure if it would be welcomed. I closed my eyes, wrapped my arms around his neck, knotting my fingers in his hair as I kissed him back. I felt his tense posture relax with my acceptance, and a single sigh of pleasure and relief escaped from him.

That single kiss felt like it lasted for hours, but actually, only a couple of minutes passed. He pulled me to him with his right arm as he released his left to the floor, pulling me out of my chair, then allowed us to gently recline together onto the rug. The moment my body was fully against his, we both tightened our hold and pulled our bodies closer together. He rolled onto his back, pulling me on top of him. As I took the lead on the kissing, he ran his fingers through my hair, gently removing the band holding my hair up. As my hair fell around my face, he ran his hands down my back and wrapped his arms around me in an extended hug, before he continued down my back and stopped on my butt. He gently squeezed with both hands and pressed my pelvis into his for a moment. I immediately felt him, hard, against me. I wanted him too... *Damn, Margo was right, I am easy*, I thought.

"What time will the girls be home?" he whispered in my ear, as I kissed his neck.

Girls? What girls?? OH... MY GIRLS!! Sweet crap, my girls!! Immediately I was back in my right mind. I placed my hands on his chest and pushed myself up, staring him in the eyes, as another question returned to my mind. I sat back, straddling him and he rose up leaning back onto his elbows, with a look of shock and surprise across his face that was caused by my sudden retreat.

"What's wrong?" he asked softly. Obviously clueless as to why I had withdrawn.

As I crossed my arms over my chest and set my face in a strong look of accusation and coming reprimand, his look became childlike. He knew he was in trouble, just no clue as to why.

"Ruh-roh... What'd I do?" he said, full voice with his eyes wide.

"It's funny you should mention my girls. Would you like to explain to me how you knew that they would be away this weekend? I had already guessed that you must have known when you planned this little trip. And now that question just confirmed my suspicion."

He looked trapped. "Um... well..."

He stammered, as I performed a flawless dismount that even an East German judge would have awarded a perfect 10 for, and sat beside him cross-legged, with my arms still crossed, my head cocked and eyebrows raised, waiting for an answer. My eyes were still fixed firmly on his, in quiet reprimand.

"Don't blame him... It was me, I contacted him first."

"HIM WHO??" My eyes flew open wide, with the realization that I had been right—someone in my own trusted inner circle was involved in this ambush.

He softly answered, "Will."

"AS IN MY BROTHER WILL?? You have got to be kidding me?!"

A feeling of total and complete betrayal washed over me. My own stinking brother, my flesh and blood, how could he set me up for this? And a bigger question and issue was how long had they been in contact with each other?

"And just how long has this little spy reconnaissance mission been in place?!"

He looked ashamed. "Since I knew for certain that my marriage was over."

"So, you could bring yourself to contact HIM but not ME?? WHAT THE HELL?? And you're expecting me to TRUST you, when you've been SCHEMING behind my back with my own damn family for MONTHS??" I could not stop my voice from being raised or shaking. I was livid.

"I didn't want you involved, until she was away from me for good. I had to continue to protect you, because you've been through enough, without her going crazy on you, again." I pushed myself up onto the ottoman and put my elbows on my knees with my forehead resting in my hands, as I stared at the floor. Will had known for *months* that the love of my life wanted to be with me... and had said *nothing*. I was going to *kill* him! My brother and I were very close. He knew every detail of what had transpired over the years between me and Jack. He had even joined in with me renaming him Jackass, by also using the name "Jack," solely when referring to him. I completely could not believe what I was hearing. I had guessed that Will was a possible avenue that Jack might choose to reach me one day, as they had known each other well in school. Because of that fact, I had made my brother swear to me that if he ever heard from him, he would tell me. Will had never broken a promise to me in his life, this was a first, and it was huge. I began searching every conversation I could remember having with my brother over the last few months, looking for any hint that he had tried to drop for me... nothing came to mind. Jack's voice snapped me back into the room, but I didn't raise my head to look at him.

"During our initial contact, I had asked him to give you a message for me, and he had immediately agreed, but went on to make it clear... frighteningly clear, I might add... that if I entered your world again, I had better be ready to see it through because he would kill me if I turned your world upside down for nothing. Then HE changed his mind and decided that it would be best if he didn't say anything to you until things were settled, especially since he lives so far away from you. I promise that's the God's honest truth... I WANTED to reach you; I didn't want to hide from you anymore! Will offered to keep in touch with me, telling me to call anytime I wanted to so he could let me know how you were, as a compromise. I was disappointed in his decision, I had hoped that he would help me safely reach you, but he's so protective of you, I had no choice but to agree to his terms, or risk Christmas being awkward for the rest of our lives."

That thought almost made me laugh, and I looked up at him. He was right, if he had gone around my brother after involving him, Will would have never forgiven him. "Protective" was a serious understatement, with regards to my brother's feelings for me. He had been that way since we were little kids, and it had grown to enormous proportions after Josh died. Even though I was older, he took his brotherly responsibility to look after me very seriously. The thought of my brother's boundless devotion to me brought an affectionate half smile to my face. Jack took it as encouragement and went on with his recollection of that first conversation with Will.

"He then openly filled me in on all that I had missed and filled in gaps of what I was only partially aware of through Facebook, over the six years that I was… away. He talked of your mental and emotional struggles, the immense heartbreak I had caused, and of your unchanging feelings for me. That only made it more difficult for me to stay away from you. I desperately wanted to make things right with you as soon as possible. I felt horrible and helpless."

He trailed off in his memory. I was still stunned and having trouble comprehending that this was all true, but I wanted to know.

"So, how often have you two talked?"

"At least every couple of weeks, sometimes in between, if I was having a bad day, or had an uneasy feeling that you weren't okay. I would have to check in, to see what was going on that had my soul aching. I was always amazed to learn that you were indeed sick or having some other stressful issue. I think it freaked Will out a bit too that I seemed to have this connection with you."

"Soulmates," I added in almost a whisper, my eyes staring off, unfocused, seeing the many times I had felt that unsettled feeling, but had been unable to discover what in his world was causing the fog.

"He's been a really good friend to me, I don't know if I could have gotten through the last few months without his encouragement and reassurance that you were okay."

I sounded almost icy in my response. "Yeah, it must have been nice to get that reassurance. Some of us just had to suffer through days like that." My eyes moved back to his and focused intensely, filled with hurt and anger again. He looked away, sensing the wrath that I was holding back.

My thoughts turned suddenly and naturally to my brother's wife, one of my best friends, and my expression changed to being appalled when I asked, "Does this mean that Faith knows, as well?" That thought was almost more unbearable than my brother keeping secrets.

"No, I really don't think so," he answered, "he didn't want to involve anyone else, knowing you would feel betrayed, as things were."

I looked away from him again and over to a picture of Faith and Will, that stood on the bookshelf, when I had a lightbulb moment… a memory of a conversation that had occurred maybe a month ago or so, with Faith.

"Well, now, that makes sense." I hadn't meant to, but I had spoken my thought out loud. He gave me a puzzled look, as I returned my eyes to his.

"What does?"

"A couple of months ago, Faith had been encouraging me to try and date again. She was concerned with the girls leaving home in the next few years that I would be lonely. She said she had discussed it with Will, and he had been REALLY against it. She couldn't get a good answer out of him, as to why he felt that way. I guess now we know."

He chuckled, "I told ya he has been a good friend, just like in high school."

I tilted my head at him with a confused look. They had known each other well enough to be considered friends back then... but "good" friends? I was missing something. He went on to explain. "Why do you think he would never leave you alone with any guy you brought home?"

I recalled the many times that someone I was dating had come to our house, and I would end up screaming at Will to go away, as he was always lurking or being downright stubborn by refusing to leave the room, claiming to have the same right to be in the den as I did, among other arguments.

"THAT STINKER!"

"He made some money, too," he admitted while nodding his head slightly.

My head lurched forward a bit as another confused, questioning look came over my face; a silent request for further clarification.

"There were a couple of guys that he actually liked. Ones he thought were good for you and that treated you well, and I had to pay him to get rid of them."

My mouth dropped open in shock. "Exactly how long did this go on?"

"For a few months after we broke up, until I resigned myself to the fact that you weren't coming back."

We sat in silence for a few minutes. I wanted to kill my brother. I was completely devastated that he had hidden this from me and could not make myself believe that he had done this. We had always told each other everything... so I thought. I felt so disappointed in him. He knew the vast depth of my love for this man, and he had let me go for months, knowing I was struggling, when I didn't have to. Just to have known that Jack was alive and well, would have been a huge burden lifted. However, I did have to acknowledge that I had hid the true depth of my ongoing grief from him for the last couple of years.

After many years of therapy, I had opened up and shared every detail with Will. Of course, he had always known that I saw Jack as "the one who got away," but previous to this admission, he'd had no idea of the true regret and magnitude of my feelings for this man. He'd become really angry; his protectiveness exploding in full glory. This had been when he joined me in calling him "Jack," and started encouraging me to "get over it, because nothing was ever going to change." I tried to tell myself that he was right, but my heart was hell bent on that not being true. So, I had tried to stop giving Will any sign that I was still struggling and put my happy face on for him. Sometimes he had still seen through my weak disguise and had tried to be supportive, but it was just easier if he stayed clueless as to the severity of my daily struggle to breathe; ignorance is bliss.

Naturally, Faith knew; women understand this heart stuff so much better than men. I had told her I didn't want my brother to know how I still felt, and she agreed it was probably for the best, as it "really ticks him off when you get down that way. He wants to defend you, and once I had to stop him from leaving, to go get in Jack's face about it." I had been surprised when she shared this with me. My little brother… still ready to beat people up to protect me. I had never mentioned it to him again, after that. And now my heart had been proven right. Things HAD changed, it WASN'T over, and Jack DID care about me. I wondered what Will thought about that? He had a big "I told ya so" coming.

For some strange reason, bringing up his and Will's agreement in high school, had made me recall one of my favorite memories from the time we had dated, and I wondered if Jack remembered it too. I had drifted away with the memory… staring, unfocused again, across the room. I discovered he had his eyes still fixed on me, when I returned my eyes to his face.

He gave me a crooked smile and asked, "What were you thinking about? Your face looked so peaceful."

I sighed and asked him, "Do you remember the time you took me for a ride on your dirt bike?" I gave him an encouraging smile.

"Yeah, I do. I should have done it more often, because it was an excuse for you to wrap your arms around me. I loved that."

"I loved that too," I agreed. "I remember I wasn't scared of falling off, or wrecking… I had complete confidence in you, and I felt so safe and happy."

"I remember at one point, you kissed my neck and I almost lost control." He laughed softly, his eyes focused on the far-off memory just as mine had been. My next thought was out of my mouth, before I realized I was saying it out loud.

"I'm so sorry I messed this up for us; it's completely my fault that we ever broke up. I had never cared for anyone… had never LOVED anyone not in my family, as much as I did you. When Josh died, I had never known the pain that comes from a love that deep, and I got scared. I never wanted to hurt like that again, so I cut you off before you could get any deeper into my heart."

He reached up, put his arms around my waist, and drug me off the ottoman onto his lap. Cradling me in his arms, he stroked my hair then kissed my forehead before he pulled me in tighter and responded. "It's good to finally have the answer to that question. However, it's not all your fault, Sunshine. We both could have done a lot of things differently. I failed you, time and time again. I'm sorry, too."

We sat like that for several minutes, with the only sound being the music coming from the TV, each song seeming to fit our situation perfectly, either past or present. Songs like "You're the Inspiration," "Can't Fight This Feeling," and "Truly" all had been staples of our teenage years and now played as a fitting soundtrack to our lives and love. "I'd Really Love to See You Tonight" must have triggered his next thought. He leaned me back slightly so he could see my face.

"I didn't come here to mess up your life. My purpose in seeing you was in hopes of finding... or rather to ask for... a place in it." His look was so sincere and heartfelt, there was no doubt in my mind that he truly felt that way.

"I know you didn't." I gave him a slight smile before I went on, "I just don't know if there's too much damage done. I'm wondering if we can even fix it. And it's just been so long." His look changed immediately from hopeful to one of pain. I continued, "Seven years ago, when we found each other again and even though we could only be friends, you PROMISED to never lose me again." I shifted to move out of his lap and slid onto the floor. "I trusted you, and you destroyed that and broke my heart." His eyes had stayed on his empty lap. He now slowly raised his head to look at me. He again licked his lips then bit into the bottom one. I could tell he was struggling to find the right words, so I went on.

"I mean, I totally get WHY you did what you did... Believe me I understand that. And I forgive you for it... I'm just not sure if I can forget it. There had to have been some way for you to keep your promise to me AND keep the peace at home. I feel like you just didn't care enough, or I wasn't important enough to you, for you to want to find that way."

He nodded silently that he understood and was acknowledging my feelings. Right on cue, Journey came in with "Send Her My Love." It was starting to be freaky. Saying those words out loud was like confirmation to me. Something clicked in my mind that totally overrode any feeling or excuse my heart could come up with. He had decided for over six years to cut me off... he had AGAIN chosen her over me, day after day. How plain did the writing on the wall have to be, before I accepted it? He had never chosen me when it came to her... Not once...

Ever. This realization clicked in my brain and suddenly I was angry again, and I had made my decision.

He still had no words as he stared into my eyes. I wanted to take his face into my hands and kiss that hurt look away. I summoned all my willpower and said, "You need to go." HIS EYES GOT HUGE. He managed to find his voice then, and the words he wanted to speak came pouring out all at once, as if a dam had opened.

"Please don't do this... I'm so sorry... I... I love you so very much. I don't want to spend another day of my life without you." He gently grabbed me by my shoulders, pleading. "You just need some more time to get used to the idea! I know this has all happened really fast for you, I just came out of nowhere... You've been on the defensive since you first heard my voice. I'm sorry that I've been pushing so hard, you need time, I get that... I can give you that, I promise, I'll be good. Just don't make a decision right now!"

Tears came to my eyes again as I gave in, taking his face into my hands. I looked so deep into his eyes, I swear I could see his soul.

"I just don't want to lead you on, to give you false hope... I just don't see us getting past this. You ABANDONED me. I can't possibly mean that much to you if you were able to walk away so easily, for so long. I love you, I do. But sometimes that just isn't enough. I can't trust you not to hurt me again. I JUST CAN'T." I leaned in and kissed his mouth softly with tears running down my face. Then I backed away, dropped my hands and whispered, "Please... just go."

He looked shocked, beaten, utterly shattered and defeated as he rose to his feet. I followed suit and stood, too, then walked past him to the door and opened it. I kept my eyes on the floor even when he paused in front of me, I didn't look up. He cupped the crown of my head in his left hand, bent his head down, and placed his lips on the top of my head and froze for a moment. He inhaled slowly, deliberately, as if taking in my scent to keep as a memory, then he kissed the top of my head and left. I didn't watch this time, I simply closed the door behind him and walked away. I picked up the remote for the TV and shut The Manhattans down in the middle of "Kiss and Say Goodbye."

I grabbed my phone, went to my bedroom, and crawled into bed. It was a little after one in the afternoon, my nap was about due. Closing my eyes did no good. All I could see was his face, no matter if my eyes were open or closed. Why didn't I have peace? My mind was finally made up. I could never trust him with my heart again, period. That was the end of the discussion! So, WHY did I feel physically ill? Where was my relief to have this chapter of my life finally closed? My head still had an aggravating dull ache. I rubbed my temples and closed my eyes. I had done the right thing, right? I began questioning myself. Replaying every moment of his visit, moment by moment, analyzing every detail. Had I done the right thing? Thankfully, somewhere in all my thoughts… sleep found me.

15

AFTERSHOCK

I wasn't really surprised when my brother called, waking me up, almost two hours later. I answered with a simple, "What?"

Will's voice came through loud, clear, and intense. "HAVE YOU LOST YOUR NATURAL MIND? WHAT THE HELL ARE YOU THINKING?? *ARE* YOU EVEN THINKING??" I was immediately fully alert, as my anger with him surfaced quickly.

"Well, if it isn't my deceitful and conniving little brother! I'm doing fine, thanks for asking!"

"Oh, don't play that crap with me. You know I did the right thing... He needed to be away from her, before we ever got you involved."

"Yeah, well..."

"Yeah, well, my ass. You know I'm right, if I had given you a heads-up, you wouldn't have been able to stay out of it, and he would have ended up losing his ass in the divorce. I did what was best for both of you! Now back to YOU... I can't believe you're doing this. After all this time, decades of loving this dude, and you send him away like it's nothing? Come on, sis, talk to me… what's going on in that head of yours?"

"When he leaves me again, it WILL kill me, this time. He broke my heart, bub, I just can't trust him with it, again."

"Bull Shit."

"Do you want me to talk to you, or not? I'm trying to be honest with you."

I heard him take a deep breath, then he replied, "I know, sis, I'm just totally floored. I thought this would be a fairy-tale ending, a dream come true. A chance for you to finally have your happily ever after, again. Never dreamed you would turn it down. Are you okay?"

"No, I'm not okay. I'm pretty sure I just made the biggest mistake of my entire life, and that's saying something, because there have been some real doozies. But I'm fairly confident in saying that I will regret this one, for the rest of my life."

"You don't HAVE to make this one. He loves you, sis. I would never have helped him get to you, if he hadn't convinced me of that."

I sighed before I responded, "I know he does. Truly I do. I'm the only one who never doubted that, remember? I TOLD you he would be back, and you told me I was full of it."

"I know, and I was wrong. I just hated seeing you alone, and at that time, I had no idea if you were right about him and didn't want to see you waste away over a daydream. You have so much to give to someone, and you deserve to be loved again. Brad would never have wanted you to spend the rest of your life alone."

"Please don't bring him into this."

"Well, it's true."

I started crying… again. "Don't cry, sis… it's gonna be okay. I think you just need some time."

"Yeah, I feel pretty overwhelmed."

"He's asked me if he should stay there, or just come home... what do you want me to tell him?"

"Yeah, he should just go. There's no sense in him being away from his life any longer than he has already. I can't trust him. He's wasting his time here."

He took a deep breath and let out a loud sigh. "I seriously saw this going so much differently... I'll tell him, but I don't think it will change anything in his mind. He will be with you or be alone... Kinda reminds me of someone else I know."

"Shut up."

He let out an exasperated chuckle. "I love you, sis. Just take your time, and really think about what you're doing, please? It's just a waste for you two to be alone, when you belong together."

"Yeah, okay, but I can't see me changing my mind. Do me a favor and let me tell Faith everything. No sense in you being in trouble with her, too."

"Oh, I'm still gonna catch hell."

"True, but maybe I can talk her down a bit for ya. I love you, bub. Talk to you soon."

"Later."

And he was gone. We had NEVER said goodbye. I guess deep down, neither of us cared for the word, ever since we had said it for the last time to Josh. I stared at my phone, knowing I needed to call Margo and Faith, but I seriously wasn't ready to be screamed at again. I decided to go take a hot bath first. The girls would be home in a couple of hours, and I looked a mess.

I filled the tub as full as possible, allowing just enough room around the rim to compensate for adding my body to it and not spill over. The water was so hot I had to ease into it a little at a time. I added some of my favorite salts for a calming aroma to fill my head and relax my overly tense muscles. When I finally managed to get my entire body into the steaming water, I closed my eyes and took a slow deep breath. My brother's voice returned to my thoughts and I had to ask myself, *Have I lost my natural mind?* Maybe I have.

Even though I had classical music playing to help calm my nerves, I could clearly hear Luther Vandross in my head, again, "just don't want to be a fool... ever again." But I couldn't fight the feeling that I was being exactly that right now, a complete and utter fool. I had loved this man most of my entire life, and here he was back... FINALLY, all mine for the taking, and I was sending him packing. *Yep, no doubt about it, you've lost your mind.* I took a deep breath and slid my head down under the surface of the water to drowned out my heart and its opinion.

As I was getting out of the tub, almost an hour later, my phone rang a familiar ringtone. "Girls Just Want to Have Fun," the one assigned to my girls, only. I wrapped a towel around me and ran to get it in the other room. It was Claire.

"Hey, Mom!" Her cheery voice immediately brightened my mood.

"Hi, baby girl, y'all on your way home?"

"Yes, ma'am, but Megan called and asked if we could spend the night with her tonight... I know we've been gone all weekend, but with summer almost over, we'd really like to go."

"Livie's okay with going too?"

Sometimes Olivia would just follow Claire's lead, not really wanting to do something, and vice versa, so I always tried to give the other one an "out." Twins were close enough, without having to feel like they were required to be joined at the hip.

"Oh, yes, ma'am, she's the one who talked me into it."

"Well, okay then, I guess I'll see you soon, when you come to grab fresh clothes and get your car?"

"Yes, ma'am, see ya soon, we love you."

"I love you more."

I hung up, glad for the extra night to get myself together but dreading not having my distractions back.

Not very long after the call they blew in and back out again, giving me big hugs and promising to fill me in on their weekend when they got home tomorrow.

I was already in my pajamas, and I had no desire to eat, so I poured myself a glass of scotch, as wine didn't provide the soothing burn that I was after. I took one slow sip as I went to my big chair to call Margo and Faith. No sense in putting it off any longer. I decided to make separate calls. I felt like one at a time was all the berating I could handle. I started with Faith, so she would have time to light into my brother, before bedtime. I had purposefully lied about trying to keep him from trouble. I wanted him to catch every ounce of hell she was going to pounce on him with. *Payback's a bitch,* I thought, as I listened to the ringing.

"Hello," she answered in her soft, sweet voice. She and my brother balanced each other out perfectly, in every way.

"Hey..." My voice broke as soon as I heard hers.

"Oh no... are you okay?"

"Yes and no... mostly, no. Honestly, I think it's possible that I've gone insane again."

"Spill it..." she commanded gently.

"I sent him away."

She gasped in shock, "NUH-UH!!"

"Yes, ma'am, I sure did. And I've pretty much been kicking myself, ever since."

"Why would you do that?! You love him, you silly goose!"

"I know!! I just can't get past him totally cutting me off, when he promised he would never leave me again. My trust in him is shattered..."

"Then start building it back from scratch!!"

"If only... Do you think it's really that easy?"

"Easier than your living out your days miserable, missing him." Ouch. She had me there. "Girl, we are the creation of a God of second chances... you should let him at least try to regain your trust, or you'll always wonder what might have happened if you *had* given him a chance! The last thing you need is more regret to carry around."

"Amen to that," I agreed before I opened the next can of worms. "And there's something else... even more trust has been betrayed."

"Oh my... go ahead..."

"I had wondered how he knew to come *this* weekend. How he knew that the girls would be away, and it turns out that he's been in touch with someone close to me for a while now. This person agreed to help him get to me, as long as it stayed a secret, and Jack agreed to stay away from me until his divorce was final."

"I kind of understand that," she began, "they were trying to protect you, that I can understand but, oh my goodness, who would do such a thing? Obviously, it couldn't be anyone who truly knew how desperate you've been to hear from him."

"Yeah... one would think... But... It was Will."

SILENCE

Can open, worms EVERYWHERE. "Faith?"

"I'm sorry... it sounded like you said it was WILL."

"I did." Silence again. "Faith??"

"I love you, girl, do the right thing. I have to go." I heard her yell, "TIMOTHY WILLIAM GRANT!!!" before the call ended.

Dead man walking, I thought. For a moment I felt sorry for my brother... A very brief moment. "Hell hath no fury like a woman scorned," or kept out of a juicy loop of knowledge. She was going to chew him up one side and down the other. I couldn't hold back the vengeful grin any longer. He was getting exactly what he deserved.

I pulled up the recent call log and touched "Margo."

"HEY!" she answered in her normal cheerful, bright voice.

"Hey, girl, how are ya?"

"Yeah, skip the formalities... did you get some?"

I had to laugh. "Just a little tongue before I sent him away."

"Well that's disappointing... WAIT, I'm sorry...YOU DID WHAT?"

"I sent him away. Told him I didn't think I could ever trust him again, then asked him to leave."

"I guess that was another way to go... really hadn't considered that route. You okay?"

"I really don't think so. I can't shake the feeling that I'm screwing up, major."

"I would have to agree."

"Thanks."

"Look, doll, I've been on this ride a long time with you. I'm fairly certain when I say that he is all you have ever wanted. I know that you were content and found a level of peace and happiness with Brad, but you were never a hundred percent all his, either. This man has had your heart from the beginning, and I doubt you could get it back from him, even if you truly wanted to." She paused to let that point hit home, then continued. "You need to seriously review the decision that you've made and be certain that you are prepared to live with it... forever. And to be honest with you... I don't think that you can, and that worries me."

"Margo... I'm terrified. There's no way I could live through him hurting me again."

"Darlin', something tells me he couldn't, either."

She was right, and I knew it. My soul had no doubts that this was all he ever wanted, too. We had finally reached the opportunity to right a great wrong, and I was too insecure to let go and let myself have the life that I personally had derailed myself from, so many years ago. Yes, he was a jackass, but he was MY jackass.

"I don't know how to fix this now... I was so cruel; you should have seen his face!

I don't know what to do."

"Do you still have a driver's license and a vehicle?"

That question seems to come from nowhere, so the tone of my reply was one of confusion. "Yeah...??"

"THEN, YOU GO AFTER HIM, YOU SILLY GIRL!"

Then it clicked. "OKAY, you're right, I can do this... I'm gonna go to him and beg him to forgive me!"

"Well I didn't say that... but at least tell him how you feel and tell him what you want."

"Okay, got it."

"Then get you some."

"STOP!" But I was able to giggle.

"HAHA!" She laughed at me. "Just trying to help you find your smile, it's gonna be okay, you got this!"

"Love you, M..."

"Love you more, NOW GO!"

I was thankful that I had not drunk any more of my scotch, so I could leave immediately, I didn't even take the time to change into real clothes. He was going to see me in the Hello Kitty pajamas the girls had given me for my birthday, as a joke. Turned out they were super comfy and I loved them. I went to my nightstand and grabbed the small box out of the top drawer. I kissed the note from the girls and put my bracelet on, then, literally running back to the living room, I grabbed my purse and went to the truck. I checked my phone while I waited for the garage door to go up. I had two texts from my brother, the first was almost two hours old and read, "I talked to him and he's leaving." The second was after I had talked to Faith and read, "Thanks a lot!" I laughed, then opened my call log and touched "Jack" as I pulled out of the driveway. I didn't even know where he was staying... It immediately went to voicemail. His phone was off. My heart sank as I put the car in drive and headed towards the restaurant he had chosen, hoping he was at one of the surrounding hotels. I then called my brother, praying he knew where to find him.

"Yeah," he answered in a very gruff voice, and I could hear Faith in the background still giving him "what for."

"I'm so sorry, bub."

"No, you're not," he replied, half tickled.

"No, I'm really not… however, I AM sorry to interrupt. I'm hoping you know where he's staying? His phone is off and I've got to find him."

"Sorry, sis." Faith's rant stopped immediately, with the realization that it was me on the phone. "He never told me where he was staying. And even if I knew, I got the impression he was leaving, just as soon as he could load up. He was devastated."

I began to cry. "I can't believe I've messed this up again… I have to find him. I'm heading your way; if I hurry, maybe I can catch him. If not, I'll be there hopefully by lunch. If you hear from him, try to get him to pull over and call me. And tell Faith I'm gonna need some clothes, cause I'm in my pajamas."

"You got it, sis, I'm proud of you… wait… Whaaa??"

I laughed and hung up.

I made a quick sweep through every hotel parking lot in that part of town, remembering how long it had taken him to get to the house in the middle of the night when he was worried. He had been close. I knew it was a long shot after what Will had said, so I wasn't surprised when I came up empty. His truck was nowhere to be found.

I called my girls and told them that everything was okay, but something had come up and I was going out of town for a few days. Liv started asking questions, and I told her I would fill in all the details when I got home, to please trust that I was alright. She finally relented. I told her I was calling their grandparents to have them either come stay with them starting tomorrow, or have them come to their house, whichever was best for them. I told her it was okay for them to call me if they needed me, and to tell her sister how very much I loved them. She sounded so confused when we hung up, but she relayed that they loved me more.

Brad's parents were also concerned that something was wrong, but I just assured them, that for the first time in a very long time, things were actually very right. I confided in them that I was headed back home to Arkansas, but not to tell the girls that detail. I promised to call them the next night, to check in, and be sure the girls were okay. They told me to be careful and reminded me that they loved me. I told them how much I appreciated their unwavering support, and that I loved them too.

I stopped for gas before getting on the interstate. I was thankful for the decline in our society's classiness, when no one gave me a second glance, since it was common to be out in pajamas these days. Sad, really, but, at the moment, it was working for me. I went inside and picked up a three-pack of energy shots, a huge bottle of water, beef jerky, and some snack mix. When I got back into the car, I plugged my phone in and cued up my music to shuffle through my entire music library, buckled my seat belt, pulled out, and got onto the interstate headed home… Home, home, Arkansas, and praying that I wouldn't have to go all the way there, or it was going to be a very long night. I took it as a sign that the very first song that my phone chose to play was "Love Will Come Back" by Chicago. I thought of the memory he had shared of that concert, and his desire to know what had caused my sudden about face of my feelings for him. I was glad that I had at least managed to answer that one question for him, after all these years. And, regardless of his offer to share in the responsibility of our demise, I still viewed the truth to be that it in no way had been his fault, the blame was all on me.

I floored it, hoping again that I could catch up to him, and hopefully not have to make the sixteen-hour drive to find him. I tried to call him again. It still went straight to voicemail. *DAMMIT. Stop being a pouty jackass and turn your phone back on! Ugh!* I thought. I knew what he was doing. He had no doubt that my mind was made up, that he had failed, and he just wanted to be alone, without interruption, while he let that sink in.

HA! I was finally doing something he didn't see coming!! He was most likely using the quiet to devise a new plan. It wasn't like him to give up so easily. I knew that somewhere in the deepest part of his mind, he was working up a new strategy. I slowed down at the state line, realizing if I hadn't caught him by now, I most likely wouldn't, unless he pulled over for an extended stop to eat, or something, he had too big of a head start. And I knew the chances of getting a ticket are higher when you were from out of state. I saved my energy shots since my adrenaline had me wide awake for now; one state down, only five more to go. I kept trying to call him. My only reward was hearing his voice each time the voicemail picked up.

I never left him a message. What was I going to say? "Hey, it's me. The dumbass that sent you away, even though she loves you more than the air she breathes... I'm chasing after you, so can you please pull over and let me catch up, so you can tell me how stupid I am, to my face?" Yeah, it was better to keep hoping he would just answer or see the missed calls when he turned his phone on and call me back. But hours passed, and neither happened. I lost count of how many times I tried to call... every five minutes it seemed like. But I could feel in my soul that he was emotionally locked down, focused on the road, and replaying the last three days in his mind, searching for what had gone wrong. I even tried the Luke and Leia thing... I concentrated as hard as I could on him (which was hard since I couldn't close my eyes) while still concentrating on the road... begging him with my thoughts, to turn on his phone. I only sensed overwhelming grief in the connection.

I had finally started to get tired, about the time I needed gas, again. Another state behind me, four more to go, and still no one even batted an eye about my attire. I purchased another huge bottle of water and went to the bathroom. I still had plenty of junk to eat, as my adrenaline rush had kept hunger at bay. My phone rang, and my heart leapt when I saw it was Will. I didn't even bother with saying hello.

"Did you talk to him?"

"No, ma'am, I was just checking on you. I can't sleep knowing that you're driving all night by yourself. You okay?"

"Yeah, I'm doing really well."

"Where are you?"

"I'm in Georgia, somewhere between Augusta and Atlanta. I just filled up, so I wouldn't have to stop in Atlanta. I'm about to slam an energy shot and get back on the road."

"Please be careful, and call me if you need help staying awake, God knows I'll be up till you get here. I love you."

"I love you more."

I hung up then reconnected my phone and got the music going again. I went with Lady Antebellum this time; I owned all their albums and knew every song on them, word for word. That should burn the time until I had to stop again somewhere close to Mississippi. I tried to call him again... nope, still straight to voicemail. I didn't let it upset me this time. I had made peace with paying the price of my penance. I would drive to Alaska to see him, if I had to. I set the cruise control to five miles over the speed limit and cracked open my first energy boost. It was going to be a really, really, long night.

I had always thought that downtown Atlanta was beautiful, especially the golden dome of the state's capital building, shining, even in the dark, just from the city lights. Each tall building, unique in its design, made the skyline distinguishable from other big cities. I had always loved big cities. After Atlanta, I felt like I was getting nowhere. The remainder of Georgia and the first leg of Alabama passed by at a crawl. I kept looking for him each and every mile. He must have literally thrown everything in the truck and left like his ass was on fire. I had thought with my SUV getting slightly better gas mileage than his truck would, I may still catch him, especially if he stopped for food. I started to consider the possibility that he had stopped for the night and made the decision that I would keep going and beat him home, if that was the case.

I had heard his voicemail greeting so many times that it was playing over and over in my thoughts, like a song stuck in my head. I was ticked that he wouldn't turn his damn phone on, then I considered that maybe it was dead. But I quickly dropped that theory, when I reminded myself that he had to have a car charger, and undoubtedly it was in the car, as he would have brought it to use on the long drive in the opposite direction. He just wanted to be alone. And with it being the middle of the night, he had no reason to suspect that anyone would be trying to call him. Birmingham was a welcome sight. It also was unique in its skyline and beautifully lit.

The mountains had crept up between the two cities and had gone mostly unnoticed in the dark. I was a huge fan of the new interstate, I-22, as it made the trip between my homes so much smoother and cut the travel time down substantially. I stopped for gas again, off the exit to Jasper. The highway that used to be my old route went through the center of the moderate-size town, and I always wondered how bad of a hit their economy had taken when the new interstate had opened. I'm sure the story was much the same as every town along Route 66, going out west. Knowing I was warming up to Mississippi, I took the opportunity, while I was stopped, to text Will with my progress. He responded that he still hadn't heard from Jack, and had tried calling several times, as well. As soon as I had made a visit to the restroom, I was on the road again.

I was really starting to fight sleep as I crossed into Mississippi, so I slammed back my second energy shot like it was tequila. Tequila was smoother, this stuff tasted totally nasty, but it never failed in fulfilling its purpose. Without even thinking about it, I touched his nickname again on my call log… no ring, voicemail, shocking.

Mississippi seemed to pass by a little bit faster. I made a mental note that I really wanted to come back to Tupelo to see "The birthplace of Elvis." The same mental note I had made every trip to, or from, home over the last 18 years. I had been to Graceland in Memphis and had even stopped with the girls a couple of summers ago on our way home, to take the full tour. But I had never visited the town of origin of the King of Rock and Roll. I love Elvis, I wondered if Jack knew that? We had so much to get to know about each other. I wasn't even sure of what his favorite color was anymore, or what he would want on a burger. Did he prefer Coke over Pepsi? He had been a Coke guy when we were kids, surely that hadn't changed. And that could be a deal breaker, I was a Coke girl, always had been. Just kidding, I would still love him, but he wouldn't be allowed to bring the competition into my house. These thoughts and questions kept my mind occupied until the sun had come up, and before I knew it, I was crossing the mighty river, with Memphis in the rearview mirror.

I hated not seeing the pyramid and Mud Island. Coming in on I-55 removed those must-see landmarks from my trip's scenery. I was thankful that with no planning or any attention to timing, I had managed to arrive after morning rush hour. The "WELCOME TO **ARKANSAS** THE NATURAL STATE, BUCKLE UP FOR SAFETY" sign felt like a greeting from an old friend. I was home. Now, I had to have a plan.

Where, exactly, was I going? I had devised several options during the trip but had kept hope alive that he would call me, before I had to choose one. He lived over an hour farther north, from my family. Did I go to my brother's and regroup? Or, should I follow him all the way home? The latter of the two ideas was a problem, as I had NO idea, other than the town of where he lived, and I was getting so tired, I was afraid the extra hour would do me in. I pulled into a busy station and truck stop in West Memphis to fill up for the final time, shot another energy gut bomb, then punched it as I returned to I-40 westbound.

I had massively exceeded the speed limit on this interstate since I was old enough to drive. I knew all of its twists and turns, and all of the state troopers' favorite hiding places along the way. I set the cruise on 85 and made like the wind. I called Will to check in, and to see what he thought was best regarding my destination dilemma.

"I don't have his address either, and I can hear that you are exhausted, so I think it's best that you come here. I'll nap until you get here, now that I know when to expect ya.

Then I'll drive you to wherever we have to go, until we find him."

Tears filled my eyes. "Thanks, bub."

"Just be careful, you're not here yet."

"Yes, sir, I love you."

"Love you more."

I touched end, then touched his name... AGAIN. *Please answer, please answer, please...* Nope. I touched the "end call" and then started my music again. I went with the Eagles, I needed something I could sing along with and that wasn't terribly slow. Before I knew it, I was past Forrest City, then Brinkley was behind me, too.

The sight of the fields was soothing. I loved the Arkansas Delta. Field after field of soy beans, rice, and milo passed by, on both sides of the interstate. My grandparents had been farmers. I loved the smell of diesel and the sight and sounds of tractors working the land.

When my brothers and I were little, our grandpa had still farmed cotton. I had wonderful memories of playing in the trailers full of white fluff and coming out with cockleburs stuck on our clothes. We had also been allowed to play in the trucks full of grain and beans, during the harvesting of soy beans and wheat. I had no memory of rolling in rice... I wondered why.

I was deep in thought, even though I was subconsciously singing aloud every song, word for word, I love the Eagles. Brad and I had seen their reunion concert in Little Rock, before we had moved to North Carolina. I was in that zone again, driving on autopilot with nothing on my radar now but my destination, and hopefully, my future. I was coming up on the Carlisle exit, when my phone rang and made me jump. Assuming it was my brother, or Faith, I didn't even look down at it and just hit the button to answer on the steering wheel.

"Hello."

I realized how tired even my voice sounded, as I cleared my throat. HIS raised voice responding, surprised me, and I physically jerked again.

"ARE YOU OKAY?"

Totally caught off guard, I couldn't find my voice in time to answer him, he sounded completely panicked.

"I had eighty-seven missed calls when I turned my phone on, and fifteen are from Will... What's wrong? Are you there? ARE YOU OKAY??"

He hadn't taken a single breath in his greeting, he was freaking out. I finally managed to speak but had to fight tears from interrupting.

"Yes, I'm here... I... I'm okay. I'm sorry if I worried you."

"YOU SCARED THE HELL OUT OF ME!"

"I'm so sorry." There was silence as I assumed he was trying to calm down. So, I tried to sound nonchalant when I asked, "Where are you?"

It took him longer to respond than it should have. I assumed he was also exhausted, and confused by my sudden interest in his whereabouts, only hours after telling him to step on out of my life. I was just about to say "hello?" to confirm he was still on the line, when he responded.

"Um…" he finally began, sounding dazed, "I just walked in the door at home. Will told me you said for me to go home."

"Yeah… I did…" Silence again. I had promised Will I would come straight to him, and I was so tired, I knew it was the best thing, but I wanted to get to him… I had to see him. I tried to keep him talking while I decided what to do. "I can't believe you drove all night. I thought maybe you would wait and leave this morning."

"Yeah, that would probably have been a better idea. I was just in shock, I guess, and didn't really think at all."

"I'm sure you're really tired then… and I should let you go."

"No, no… I'm good. You must have something on your mind, since you've been

up all night trying to call me. Were you not able to sleep? Talk to me, Sunshine."

I really didn't want to apologize over the phone. I wanted to look him in the eyes, and for him to see the sincerity in mine, when I told him I had been wrong and ask him if he would consider forgiving me for my stubbornness. It occurred to me that I was about an hour from my brother's; actually, a little less.

His voice came again: "Really, it's okay, whatever it is, PLEASE just talk to me."

"I know that I have no right to ask, but, I need you to do something for me."

"ANYTHING, name it and it's yours, even if it's getting back in the truck and coming back to you."

"I know you're exhausted, I would never ask THAT, but can you go to my brother's house, please?"

"You mean, now?"

"Yes, right now... he has something for you. And I really want you to have it, as soon as possible."

"What is it?"

"It's something that belongs to you... please. I need for you to have everything back that is yours, so we can move on."

"What if I don't want to move on?"

"Just go and get all that is yours, then it's up to you what you want to do... Move on... don't. That's your call, and your call only, to make. Please, it's very important to me, and it would mean everything to me if you would go." Silence... I hated to play this card, but he was being difficult. "You said ANYTHING, and you would do it."

He exhaled, then asked, "Can I shower first?"

"No." I'll be damned if he gets a shower, and I show up in my pajamas. So, I came up with the best excuse I could think of quickly. "Will was willing to go into work later, so he's home and will be waiting for you, so the sooner you can get there, the better... so he can get on into work. I'll let him know that you're on your way. Do you know where you're going?"

"They built on the family farm, didn't they?"

"Yes, I'm sure you'll have no problem finding their huge house once you pull onto the property."

"Okay, Sunshine. I'll leave right now."

"Great, I'll call now and let him know that you're on your way... and thank you."

"Always."

I hung up and called Will... I had a new plan.

16

HOMECOMING

Seeing downtown Little Rock made me feel all warm inside, as it did every time I came over the Arkansas River Bridge. On my left, the Clinton Library was supposed to resemble a bridge to the future or something, but it looked like a glass double-wide trailer parked on the bank of the river. And to my right, off just a bit in the distance, was our State Capitol Building, which is a perfect replica of the national one. I exited onto I-630 to cut over to the west side of town. I could drive this stretch of road in my sleep, which may have come in handy before, but since his call, I had enjoyed a new rush of energy and adrenaline.

I was wide awake but could not ignore the fatigue in my body. I was running on fumes. At Shackleford Rd., I exited onto I-430, and headed south to Col. Glenn. I was getting close. It always amazed me how much this area had changed since we were kids. It was all completely built up now with stores, restaurants, and car dealerships but had been mostly all wooded area, then, with just one corner store with a couple of gas pumps near our high school. I missed the simple beauty of the undeveloped land. I hit exit number 4 and went west; I was home.

I was still rushing to beat Jack to Faith and Will's, so I slid into my brother's driveway on two wheels, throwing gravel a good eight feet. I knew I would only have a few minutes to get my car around back and hidden, before he pulled in behind me, maybe 20 minutes at the most, if I was lucky. I pulled around back, finding Will and Faith standing in the driveway, motioning for me to pull into the garage. I rolled in, and they put the door down as soon as I cut the engine. I got out, and my brother's arms were wrapped tight around me.

"This may be the dumbest stunt you've ever pulled. Traipsing across half the dang country in the middle of the night, in your damn underwear! You HAVE lost your marbles." He released me and I took the couple of steps to where Faith was waiting patiently with her arms out, ready for her turn to hug me.

As we hugged she said, "We put you in the garage, on the off chance he pulls around back when he gets here."

I turned to ask Will, "Have you heard from him?"

"Yeah, he sent me a text message saying that he hoped I was aware that he was on his way. I told him yes and gave him some details on finding the house."

"Thanks."

Faith grabbed my hand and pulled me into the house, saying, "Girl, let's at least try and do something with that head, before he gets here!"

I laughed. "Good luck with that." I knew that after being up over 30 hours, there wasn't much anyone could do to make me presentable. But it was what it was, at this point. "And coffee?" I asked.

"Of course, there's coffee!! I'm on my fourth pot!" my brother boomed with pride.

Will needed a coffee intervention. If you searched "Mr. Coffee" on the internet, a picture of my brother came up. His addiction had become a running family joke.

I apologized to my brother for making him miss work. He hugged me again and laughed. "What good is it to own your own company, if you can't ditch when ya want to? What are they gonna do? Fire me? BWAHAHAHAHA!!!"

I had to laugh, too. I never realized how much I missed my family, until I was home with them. Even after all the years I'd spent in North Carolina, THIS was still home. Faith sat me in a chair at the snack bar and headed down the hall. Will poured me a huge mug of coffee and set it on the counter in front of me. Taking it into both hands, I held it under my nose to let the aroma hit my senses, and hopefully, trigger some alertness to fire. Faith soon returned with her hair stuff.

Will exclaimed, "Oh good grief! Honey, she's not entering in a pageant!"

"I KNOW, it was just easier to bring it all than to pick through it, we have no time!"

I had to giggle at them. I was so tired that the sillies were starting to come on.

"Seriously," I said. "Let's just brush it back into a ponytail. I'll even let you use a matching pink scrunchie."

"Oooooo, we're going all out!!" Faith said as she laughed, teasing me. I took a huge drink of my coffee.

"You're not CHANGING?" Will asked, obviously shocked and horrified by the revelation.

"No. I doubt there's time anyway."

Faith added, "She looks precious, and she's covered, it isn't like she's in a teddy."

I took down another huge gulp of coffee as Will rolled his eyes at us, and Faith snapped a scrunchie in place. My thinking had only begun to sharpen just as the dogs started barking, and we could hear the gravel crunching under the incoming vehicle. I set my coffee down on the counter and looked at my brother, as I felt all the blood drain from my face.

Will took my hand and squeezed it, as he looked me in the eyes. "I'll go out first. You hang back for a bit."

That was a great idea, because I was now shaking like a leaf and had a sudden urge to vomit. Probably more from the effect of my brother's diesel-grade coffee, but my nerves weren't helping. I looked at Faith, with tears quickly filling my eyes.

"What if I hurt him so bad that he doesn't want me, now?"

She answered in her soft, always understanding tone, "Honey, he wouldn't be here, if he didn't still want you. I think him coming here is a sign of him clinging to any piece he still has left of you."

I nodded, and she wiped the tears that fell briefly down my cheeks. Thank God they hadn't brought friends, or the snot, this time. It was just the few.

Smiling, Faith added, "Good thing we didn't have time for makeup, it would have been ruined before you even make it to the porch." I smiled as I took a deep, slow breath in through my nose, as we went to where we could see and hear what Jack and Will were saying, but where we could remain unseen.

We reached our perfect spot to spy, just as Will was calling off the dogs, and Jack was stepping out of his truck. I could tell immediately from his face that he was obviously exhausted, especially around his eyes, they were almost black. He stopped at the front of his truck, as Will had left the porch and was walking out into the yard to meet him. Jack spoke first.

"Hey, man, how's it going?"

"It's good... nice truck!"

I looked at Faith and said, "You have GOT to be kidding me, we're gonna admire vehicles, at a time like this?"

She laughed almost silently, and said, "Men."

We both shook our heads and returned our attention to the yard. They had shaken hands as Jack had thanked him, and then there was babble about fuel mileage, the tire size, and the power of the wrench. *Just shoot me, can we get on with this*?? I thought. My brother was probably enjoying dragging this out, as payback for the punishment he had endured from Faith over his secret keeping.

"Man, speaking of mileage, I can't believe you drove all night… only a CRAZY person would do that!"

He managed to look back towards the house with his statement, as it was truly aimed at me and said purely for my benefit, I knew. Faith rolled her eyes at me. Jack's voice sounded as exhausted as he looked.

"Yeah, I had a lot to think about, so it really went by pretty fast, wasn't too bad, no traffic at all… but I'm sure ready for a nap now, no lie."

"I can imagine," Will responded. There was a moment of awkward silence before Jack pressed forward…

"She told me that YOU have something for me, something that **belongs** to me? I can't imagine what she's talking about, she must be mistaken…"

I looked at Faith. "Here we go."

Will looked back towards the house. "Yes, I sure do. There's no mistake, wait here." He started walking back towards the house and called, "FAITH?"

She hugged my neck as she answered loudly, "Coming!"

She went to the huge screen door, pushed it open and walked out onto the porch; then she stepped to the side and held it open, so I could follow. I took a deep breath and held it, as I walked out of the shadows of the inside of the house and onto the sun-filled porch. Still feeling unsure about what his reaction was going to be, I bit my lip as I raised my head to see his face. I bit down so hard, I'm surprised I didn't taste blood. He looked directly into my face but seemed dazed and confused, like he'd been hit over the head with a large bat, or perhaps a cast iron skillet. He didn't move.

My brother had stopped at the bottom of the three steps off the porch, on his walk to fetch me. Will looked back at Jack with a huge knowing smile, and asked, "This IS yours, right?"

Faith was following me as I lowered my head again, and went slowly down the stairs, almost as slow as a small child... taking them one at a time, hanging each foot in mid-air for a moment over each upcoming step. I confirmed, by raising only my eyes, that he STILL had not moved from the front of his truck. I took the final step to the ground, and Faith took my hand as she settled in beside me.

"I told you I really screwed up, bub. He doesn't want me, now," I said, so softly that only they could hear me, as my eyes filled with tears again. I stopped next to Will, who still hadn't taken his eyes off Jack, and looked to my brother's face. He was still staring at Jack, with the same knowing grin on his face.

"Hell yes, he does."

Turning my head to trace my brother's stare, I met Jack's eyes again; they were now open wide. I half expected to hear an audible "click" as his mind cycled through the surprise, comprehension and confirmation that I was, indeed, standing there. In a split second, he bolted from the side of the truck towards the house, and before I even knew what I was doing, I was in a full sprint across the yard towards him, too. I leapt up into his arms and wrapped my arms and legs around him.

"You're here... I can't believe you're here," he said softly in my ear.

I pulled back just far enough to look into his eyes, our noses were almost touching. Holding me with only one arm, he stroked my head with his other hand, but still looking bewildered, he spoke again. "How? Why?"

"I drove all night too, trying to catch you, as soon as I realized that I'm an idiot."

Placing his hand on my forehead, he pushed all the wispy hairs back away from my face, as he looked deep into my eyes. "No, I'm an idiot. I should have left my phone on."

I smiled and rubbed noses with him. "You ARE an idiot."

His eyes sparkled and we both laughed lightly, as we held each other's gaze. I released my legs from around his waist, and he allowed me to stand but kept his left arm around my waist and rested his right hand on my hip. I stood looking into his eyes, thrilled to be inside the loose embrace, with my right hand resting on his left shoulder and my left one on his chest. I could feel his heart beating, and that made my whole day. He moved his hand from my hip and took my hand from his chest, into it. That's when he noticed that I was wearing his bracelet. He stared into my eyes with a look of disbelief, and that perfect crooked smile that made my heart do flips. He softly kissed my wrist and then the bracelet.

"So, what's the plan?" he asked.

"Well, I know it sounds like a **really** crazy and pretty farfetched idea, but Faith seems to think that we should simply start over."

He looked up over my head at Faith and gave her a smile of thanks that made a silent promise that he owed her the world. Whatever you want, I'll do," he said, and as he returned his eyes to mine, I smiled shyly.

"I think it's a good plan. It's simple and easy to remember." I smiled and winked at him, continuing, "We need to start rebuilding our trust. And we need to get to know each other again. It dawned on me last night that I don't even know your favorite color anymore."

He sighed and moved our hands directly over his heart. "It's green. And I promise I will NEVER intentionally do anything that might hurt you, ever again."

I searched his eyes for a moment, then replied, "Well... I guess that's a start." He smiled at me with the sweetest, most relieved smile. "So... shall we officially kick off our do-over?" I asked as I pulled my hand from his, dropped my arm from his shoulder, and pushed back a half step.

He cocked his head, and a look of exhausted confusion flooded his eyes. He would need some of Will's coffee, and soon. He was struggling to keep up with me, in my caffeine boosted state. I extended my right hand towards him.

"Hi, I'm Abigail Grant. People who love me just call me Abbi."

He laughed out loud and the sound of his relief filled the air, as he accepted my hand with his right one.

"I'm Cole Ward. It's very nice to meet you... ABBI."

As we shook hands, staring into each other's eyes, Faith yelled out, "ARE YA GONNA KISS HER OR NOT??" My mind began playing the Thompson Square song.

He chuckled as he looked over at her, and answered, "HEY, GIVE ME A BREAK! WE JUST MET!" That made me giggle, and his eyes returned to mine, lit up like fire from the sound.

"Kiss me, Jack."

His eyes widened with shock and confusion, as he repeated, "Jack??"

WHOOPS

"It's a long story," I said, with a guilty smile.

"Well... we have plenty of time for you to tell me it later."

Then he put his arms around my waist, lifting me off the ground, as he placed the sweetest, most sincere kiss on my lips that I had ever been given. I put my arms around his neck, knotting my fingers in his hair as I parted my lips and returned the gesture.

Epilogue

BEGINNING

It's been two and a half years since we shook hands and started fresh. The girls graduated last May and indeed managed to stay together for college. They settled on the University of North Carolina because of in-state tuition and to be close to Brad's parents. Also, several of their friends were going there too. The Coopers decided to keep their café at least until the girls finished college, and then they would look into retiring and traveling. The girls and I were thrilled that they were excited to attend, today. They had gotten to know Cole and expressed to me that they viewed me as forever being their daughter and wanted nothing less for me than a joy-filled life. They were also certain that I had Brad's blessing, along with their own. We cried together, and I thanked them, once again, for their never-yielding support over the last 10 years since Brad's death.

I had not allowed Cole to move, to be with me... "It's less than two years, we'll make it work," I insisted. We stockpiled a ton of airline miles, as a LOT of flying had occurred. Being apart made us both miserable and was almost unbearable, so we were constantly trying to get to the other one. Owning his own business allowed him to take long weekends. And I could go home to visit, for as long as breaks in the girls' schedule would allow. He came to us most of both football seasons, to support the girls in their dance performances.

My girls… I have no words for how amazing my girls have been. When I called them shortly after we came inside from Will's yard that day, they squealed and cried with excitement that I had finally reunited with Cole. They insisted on speaking to him and made him promise to return as soon as possible, so that they could meet him properly. They stole his heart immediately with their unconditional acceptance, exuberant joy in our reunion, and their obvious deep love and devotion for me. From that moment on, he has been wrapped around their little fingers. His kids gave me a warm welcome as well, expressing their wish for their dad to be as happy as their mom finally seemed to be. I adored his kids, they were smart, funny, and loving… all the best parts of their dad. His parents were thrilled to learn the news, and his mom swore me to secrecy, sharing that she had NEVER cared for Cole's previous choice, and that she was delighted to have me back.

After the girls graduated, we sold the house and any furniture that didn't have sentimental value. We left the rest in storage, until we knew where it needed to be delivered. Cole made his last trip out to see us, to celebrate the girls' 18th birthday. He gave them each charm bracelets much like mine. Each had three charms, one with Brad's and my birthstones in a heart together with theirs, an infinity sign to symbolize Cole's promise to be there for them forever, and another heart with their monogram engraved on it in elegant script. He loaded up my truck for the drive to Arkansas and flew back to await our arrival; as the girls had forbid him to crash our last girls' road trip. They were thrilled that we were going to be home in time to attend our family's annual Independence Day picnic on the farm and would get to see their cousins before going back to North Carolina to start school. They were excited that they would be able to help me find somewhere to live and settle a bit before they had to fly back. I promised them that I would fly in to see them as often as they wished, but I was already dreading them being so far away. However, my beautiful birds were ready to fly, and I was excited to watch them soar.

On the 4th, we arrived at Will and Faith's early, to help set up and to be ready to greet the guests when they began arriving. We were staying with my parents, so my momma loaded us down with the food she had ready to send, and other items that Faith requested to borrow. As we were unloading, Cole pulled up; his truck loaded with folding chairs. The girls ran to greet him, and he hugged them as tight as I had watched him hug his own kids. Then he walked to me and kissed me like he hadn't seen me in months, instead of just the night before.

SWOON

We managed to have everything set up shortly before the guests began arriving, and the evening passed swiftly with food, music, and laughter. Before we knew it, the sun had set, and Will was calling for everyone to head out to the pasture to watch the fireworks. Cole surprised me when he scooped me up and carried me out to the most remote corner, away from the crowd. He set me down facing him and ran his hands through my hair, pushing the curls back away from my face.

"I love you, Abbi. I hope that I have managed to prove that to you, by now."

"You have… I have no doubt of that in my mind, now. And I love you, more than ever."

His fingers were still knotted in my hair, twisting the curls between his fingertips, as his hands rested on my shoulders. He looked deep into my eyes, and leaned down to kiss me, just as the first fireworks exploded, lighting up the clear night sky and making his eyes sparkle. He followed the big kiss with two small, quick, soft ones, then pulled back, took a deep breath as he removed something from his pocket, and went down on one knee. My heart started racing… THIS WAS HAPPENING!!! He took my left hand into his right, and presented a very elegant, beautiful, antique-style ring, in his left. The center diamond made me question if Queen Elizabeth was missing a crown jewel.

"Abigail Grant, I have waited most of my life to ask you… if you would do me the honor of spending the rest of your life with me. I can't imagine mine without you now… Will you marry me?"

Happy tears began to run down my cheeks, as I gave an attempt at smiling. But we all know a crying smile is never pretty, so I covered my mouth with my right hand and began to nod as I managed to softly say, "Yes," as my voice broke with the sobs I was holding back. He slid the ring on my finger, jumped up, and lifted me off my feet in a huge bear hug. With my chin resting on his shoulder, I opened my eyes and discovered in the light of the fireworks that my entire family was facing us, watching. My daddy slapped my brother on the back, wearing a huge grin, and my girls were in tears too, along with my momma and Faith.

The eight months that followed had flown by.

It's a beautiful spring day in March. The Bradford pear and redbud trees are in full bloom, along with the deep-pink azalea bushes that Faith lovingly planted around the yard, before she and Will had even finished building the house, two decades ago. She also planted an insane amount of additional blooming plants early this season, in the hopes of adding even more color to the landscape for my big day. It had worked to perfection. My brother's ranch was so washed in color, it looked like Walt Disney had thrown up everywhere. Okay, to keep it classy, it rivaled a Monet painting… It's breathtakingly beautiful. The ceremony is to be in the open air, under a massive oak tree, where a heavily floral-wrapped arbor is standing in front of several rows of white wooden chairs. My daddy and brother made the arbor together, and it is a gift to be placed in the backyard of the new home that Cole and I have picked out, together.

The huge white tent that stands several feet away is lit inside with thousands of white Christmas lights and is filled with decorated tables covered in assorted pastel-colored tablecloths. It looks like we are expecting the Easter Bunny, but it is beautiful. There is a dance floor in the center and a DJ set up on the left side, as you enter. Everyone will enter from the end closest to the ceremony area, so the food and all-important cake table are set up opposite from there. More importantly, the bar is just inside the door and to the right, anchored at one end by a champagne fountain.

I'm not lying when I say this tent is HUGE. I teased Faith and told her they should keep it and start running a circus in it. Initially, we had only invited our immediate family and close friends but had later decided it would be fun to add our entire high school class. We were humbled by how many classmates had RSVP'd, and we were expecting about half of those that graduated with us, in addition to their "plus ones," making our small affair explode into a full-out extravaganza with over 200 guests. Faith had been delighted when I agreed to let her go all out and hire a party planner.

Faith made Will clean up the barn to use as the "staging area" for the groom. She even made Bubba bring in floor covering for the concrete floor. He had managed to get away with green "turf," insisting it was a "guy thing." Don't get the wrong idea when I say "barn," this thing is nice, and complete with air-conditioning, and "his" and "her" restrooms. We used it for family picnics like the 4th of July, as it has several bay doors that open making it feel more like a pavilion. Cole thought it was perfect. He was glad to be away from the house, as the HighLites had threatened him within an inch of his life, if he were to try to see the bride before I hit the aisle. Margo and Courtney had promised they would "cut him" if they saw him set so much as a toe on the porch, and Sarah and Savannah had gladly promised to hold him down, while they did.

I can see him from the window of the upstairs bedroom I'm using as my dressing room. And I have been scolded several times to "snap out of it," and pay attention to my assistant's many instructions and questions. The last time I peeked, I had witnessed my daddy walking out towards the pond with Cole at his side, and my daddy had that same look he always had whenever I was picked up for a date, when I was a kid. Faith walked up beside me, and noticing what I was watching, commented, "Well, that should be fun… God bless him." And we both giggled, as she took my hand and guided me to the "hair station."

It was a good thing the bedrooms in my brother's house were large, as I was surrounded by my five closest friends, my girls, who were on spring break, and my momma. Along with the hair station, there was also a table loaded with makeup, my attire was arranged across the bed, and Faith had set up a mini bar, "just in case our nerves start to get the best of us." I, however, had not touched a drop. The HighLites were already deep into the wine, but I have never felt calmer or more at peace, in my life. I am excited, of course. But not in any way, shape, or form, am I nervous. As my hair and makeup was declared finished, Sarah's face lit up with her beautiful smile, as she proclaimed, "Girl, it's time to get you dressed!" Courtney added, "Yeah, bitch, let's get this show on the road!" We had lovingly begun calling each other "bitch" a decade ago, on one of our weekends. MAINLY, 'cause we couldn't do it without giggling.

I stand and walk over to the bed, where my dress has been lovingly spread out by my baby girls, to keep it from wrinkling. I've gone with an antique white and style. It's simple, form fitting, and elegant. The color had reminded Will of Yarnell's Homemade Vanilla ice cream.

I'm now standing at the foot of the bed, staring at the dress. "Wow… Never thought I'd ever wear another one of these."

Courtney responded first, but just by a hair ahead of Margo, so it was ALMOST in unison, when they said: "We could send you down naked."

Everyone in the room laughed, and laughed hard, more from the appreciation that we all thought alike than from the actual implication. I take a slow, deep, breath and let it out as I drop my robe and hold my arms out in a silent request to be handed my dress. Olivia picks it up, and Claire unzips it, as they both hold it down for me to step into. My momma steps in and zips me in. Shoe selection had been an ordeal, as we knew that heels of any height wouldn't be wise on the uneven terrain that waited outside, so we had gone with a turn-of-the-century style boot, with a block heel. They complemented the dress design perfectly.

We were all about to head down, when Claire exclaims, "WAIT, MOMMA!! We almost forgot the something blue!!" And she darts to retrieve the light-blue garter from the hair table.

"Your brother has dared Cole to remove it with his teeth. He promised to pay him a hundred dollars, if he'll do it," Faith shared.

"He's trying to give Daddy a stroke," I answered, shaking my head.

"I've got a twenty that says Cole does it," Margo challenges.

"I'll take that action," my momma replies. "That boy is still scared to death of her daddy."

We all giggle again and head downstairs to wait for my daddy to come fetch me, for our walk together down the aisle. The others kiss me for luck, as they leave me in the living room and go outside to find their seats. The girls go ahead and stepped out onto the porch, as they are my maids of honor and will lead the way, just as my daddy comes to the door to escort me.

"You ready, baby girl?"

"Oh, yes, sir. More than you know."

"It's been a long time coming, I know. To be honest, when you dated in school, I always thought he would be the one. You really shocked me and your momma when you broke up with him…" he trailed off and looked me in the eye. "But you did okay for yourself, you made a good life with Brad, and gave me some beautiful grandgirls. I'm proud of you, Abbi, and I love you, more than I can tell ya."

"I know, Daddy… I love you more." He kissed my forehead, just as the girls squealed. "It's time!!"

They step off the porch together, in their matching periwinkle-blue sundresses, hand in hand, and holding their flowers in the other hand, while smiling ear to ear. Daddy and I step onto the porch and the light breeze begins tossing my curls around.

"You look beautiful."

"Thank you, Daddy."

We start our slow walk across the yard. I had not wanted the traditional "Here Comes the Bride" as this was not our first rodeo, and in its place, I had chosen "I'm Yours" by Jason Mraz, and it cues up the moment we make our appearance at the end of the aisle. Cole is listening to Will, his best man, whisper something to him, but turns to face me at the start of the music. His face lights up like it had that day in the yard, when it finally clicked that it was indeed me, standing before him. We never take our eyes off each other as I make my way to his side.

The preacher asks, "Who gives this woman?"

My Daddy's voice actually cracks when he responds, "Her mother and I do." I turn my head to his face and see tears welled up in his eyes. He extends my hand to Cole and looks him dead in the eyes.

"It's about damn time, boy."

"Yes, sir, it sure is."

"You be good to my girl now..." Cole nodded to him, as Daddy turns and takes his seat next to Momma. Cole looks down at me and gives me my favorite crooked smile, as he winks at me. I smile back up at him, as we turn to finally publicly vow to spend forever together.

We decided to keep the ceremony traditional and simple. After considering writing our own vows, we both realized the high probability that neither of us would make it through reciting them without crying, which would make it impossible for our guests to understand a word we were saying. We both begin crying anyway, with the basic "repeat after me version" but the tears evaporate quickly, when permission to "kiss your bride" is given. And, what a kiss! Cole pulls me in as close as he can get me, and presses me against his body, while lifting me off my feet at the same time. I wrap my arms around his neck, as he parts his lips and places his mouth on mine. Just for Margo, I lightly brush my tongue against his, as our mouths melt together in this perfect, beautiful moment. With the encouragement of our guests' verbal approval and applause, Cole tilts his head in the opposite direction and extends the show, as we both get tickled, giggling a little. We pull back slightly, and he returns my feet to the ground.

The preacher clears his throat and chimes in, while laughing, "Well, then!!" We turn to face the crowd as they join in our laughter, as he continues, "Now, it's my pleasure to introduce to you for the first time... Mr. and Mrs. Cole Ward!"

A loud, unanimous cheer erupts from our guests and Barry White's voice fills the air singing "You're the First, the Last, My Everything" as we begin our stroll, arm in arm, back down the aisle, heading into our long-awaited happily ever after.

ABOUT THE AUTHOR

A. B. Wood is a sassy southern girl with a love for people, food, music and laughter; and will never turn down a glass of wine or whiskey. Being an only child, raised by a single mom, and a wife and mother of two boys, she has experienced so many "ya can't make this stuff up" moments in her life, it just made sense to start writing. Her favorite season is college football (GO HOGS) and her happy place is on any beach. When she's not writing you can find her volunteering at her local high school. In her free time, she enjoys watching movies and historically based television series, reading and traveling. Her motto is, "Don't miss out on living, 'cause you're afraid of dying."

Follow A. B. Wood on:

> Facebook: facebook.com/writergirl1987
>
> Twitter: twitter.com/writergirl1987
>
> Instagram:
> instagram.com/writergirl1987/

Made in the USA
Middletown, DE
22 May 2018